Iceberg
by Paul Kavanagh
Honest Publishing

All Rights Reserved
© Copyright 2011 Paul Kavanagh
ISBN 978-0-9571427-0-1

Manufactured in the United Kingdom
Cover and Illustrations: Alex Chilvers

m

Iceberg
Paul Kavanagh

GOING DOWN

They were poor and defeated and they scurried through life, they feared the light, they feared the heel of a size ten boot, they feared their own shadows, shadows which had been distorted, as two cockroaches.

They lived in a grim Northern town.

It had been shaped by the wind and the rain, by the screams, the cries, the punches and the kicks, the shattered glass that covered the roads, the vandalized shutters, the bars on shop windows and pubs, the flashing lights and sirens, the fear, the paranoia, the hatred, the abuse, the abandonment, the mildew, the mold, the moss, the smell of verdigris that soiled, by the nodes of wasteland that housed the homeless, by the failures and the diseased, by the imprisoned and the unemployed.

Its streets were narrow and winding, the backstreets dark and dangerous.

It was a redbrick Northern town tenaciously fighting off a slow death, a death that was inevitable, death was near, the fighting was now most brutal, the town was now at the stage where death glowed neon.

The Northern town and the people were fighting with all

they had; they were steadfast, obdurate, and blind.

This fight had left scars upon the people's faces. The scars varied. The scars deformed, the scars cut deep, the scars never closed they hemorrhaged obscenities perpetually, loudly, making up new obscenities when the old obscenities were deemed mundane and harmless, the scars would never heal; the scars were passed down from mother to daughter from father to son.

To alleviate the pain and suffering violence and boredom all turned to alcohol and drugs and cigarettes and passionless sex.

Lies and deceit were as common as the red house brick; violence and thievery were as common as the dog excrement left on the uneven pavements.

Mothers found comfort in prams with puling babies and fathers vented in flashes of gratuitous, mindless violence. Mothers were superseded by daughters and fathers were superseded by sons, the circle just kept turning, and the perpetrators kept perpetrating, the scars got longer and deeper.

The rented flat was deep within a council estate. Sometimes the drunks on their way home from the local pub - a pub that Don and Phoebe never went to, it was run down and the windows had bars, there were more fights than singsongs - shouted obscenities. The obscenities were thick as the clouds that hung inert over the grim Northern town and as plentiful as the rain that covered the red bricks in green, slimy moss. Don and Phoebe were unsure if the obscenities were meant for them. The obscenities could have been for anybody, but they did grow louder and viler as the drunks staggered past

Don and Phoebe's flat. The rented flat they shared was small. All the furniture was secondhand or homemade. It was an incongruous place, uncomfortable, porous, and unwelcoming. Don and Phoebe did their best to make it feel like home, but it was too much for them, the flat would always feel as though it belonged to somebody else. Don did his best to keep the flat clean. He kept the sink clear of dirty pots; he hoovered when the hoover worked; he removed the dust and the dead skin and the discarded hairs. He tried. A flower and herbs sat on the windowsill in the kitchen. Don watered the flower and herbs, but he knew they were dying, if not already dead. They lacked sun, there was no warmth, and the water smelt of rust.

A dog shared the rented flat. It lived on scraps and generic dog food. It struggled not to be taken outside and once outside it whined to be taken back indoors. The dog no longer barked. It was an emaciated thing, ugly, and feeble of mind. The dog was found on a street corner. A car had hit the dog. Don and Phoebe had been to the pictures. At the time Don was working at a music store and Phoebe was teaching English. The dog was whimpering. There was nothing broken. The dog had a fever and was drenched; it smelt of the water that trickled through the canal, verdigris, rotten eggs, carrion. They agreed that they should take the dog home. On the collar there was no name or address. Not wishing to impose on the dog they agreed not to give the dog a new name. The dog already had a leash, which was made of old rope; they untied the brick from the old rope and took the dog home. The dog filled out quickly. They saw psychological damage. A knock on the door sent the dog hiding. If something was dropped or if there was a loud bang the dog defecated.

The flat's electrics smoked and blew. The dog defecated a lot.

The shower screamed as though the hot water was scalding. After much screaming the shower would cry as it bled. At night the drops hitting the iron bath grew louder.

Burglars had been and gone and had decided to leave with nothing. They had kicked in the front door and the footprints on the front door resembled cave art. Don and Phoebe didn't remove the footprints, they appreciated the art, and somehow they deterred other burglars.

The landlord was a local villain with a bushy moustache and a very short temper. He had a full head of jet black hair that matched his long leather jacket. He wore white trainers and an array of gold rings and necklaces. Once a month he would turn up at the flat and fix something that did not need fixing. He was always vexed, scowling, and caustic. Don and Phoebe tried to keep out of his way. He would sit in the front room and put his feet up onto the precarious coffee table. He took up the whole couch. Don was made to sit on the floor; Phoebe was banished to the kitchen.

The landlord could put up with Don, but the sight of Phoebe enraged him. It was the school teacher face, and he hated school teachers more so than the police.

He painted over the radiators with white paint and called the old radiators new. They could not use the radiators; the fumes that exuded from the newly painted radiators were poisonous. He charged Don and Phoebe for his time and labor.

He nailed the windows shut and called it crime prevention, after Don and Phoebe pleaded and begged, he removed the nails and charged them for both jobs.

He left nail clippings on the coffee table. He picked his nose, rolled the snot into balls and aimed the balls of snot at the television. He filled the air with his insides and looked at Don with disgust. He spat onto the electric rings in the fireplace and laughed when his phlegm defeated the electric rings.

The landlord was not a man to be messed with; his face, hands and tattoos advertised this fact. On his neck was a tattoo of a mad dog. The dog was shown to be rabid. It frothed at the mouth, and its eyes were bloodshot. When the landlord laughed the mad dog barked.

The rent was always paid on time.

When the landlord was in the flat he spent many hours on the telephone. Don would sit crosslegged. He would attack his nails.

"I bit his ear off." Here the landlord would laugh, the mad dog bark, and Don would think about crawling under the carpet and staying there, crawling with earwigs, living off cockroaches.

The landlord had a way with words, he could twist them, contort them, benign words found new connotations, the words were animated, a movie was projected into the head of Don. It was a very violent movie. Only a spliff and a mug of tea would expel the images.

The local drug dealer, who lived three doors up and had had his door kicked in more by the drug squad than the burglars, berated Don and Phoebe for the paltry weights they bought; he liked Don's paintings and so still sorted them out.

The landlord was unaware of the dog. The dog was a much better judge of character than either Don or Phoebe.

"You people really need to start using deodorant," said the landlord.

One morning while sat on the toilet Don looked down between his opened legs and through the slits in the wooden floor saw the top of the head of the man underneath. The man was struggling to brush his teeth.

The landlord shrugged his shoulders and laughed. He sat down and put his feet up on the precarious coffee table. "Make us a brew," said the landlord. He would drink seven to eight cups of tea and he would eat half a loaf of bread, toasted and buttered. "You really need to get a computer," said the landlord. He didn't rent out computers. If he did Don and Phoebe would have had a computer. Don made a cup of tea and toasted three slices of bread. The landlord picked up the phone and dialed. "Did you get it?" He waited. "Good. Wait" - Don handed the landlord his mug of tea - "put the toast on the table and leave the room, important business to discuss." From the bedroom Don could hear the landlord's business. After the phonecall the landlord called for Don. He wanted a cup of tea and more toast. It was a busy morning. The landlord was involved in many things. He knew a lot of people and a lot of people knew him. Don wished he had never met the landlord. Don or Phoebe had been introduced to the landlord via the Town Council. The landlord bought a number of properties from the Town Council on the cheap, the Town Council wanted to rid themselves of dilapidated housing, cantankerous tenants, a myriad of problems, and the landlord no longer wanted the appellation of drug dealer and pimp, and so Don and Phoebe had a new landlord. They had spent ten years in the flat under the Town Council and so the landlord offered them another ten-year contract. They had to sign.

"What's that?" asked the landlord. He held up a big book Phoebe had bought at the library. The book was about architecture. "It's a big book. I would love to see you read that," said the landlord. It was not a joke; he really wanted Don to read the book. He drank the tea, finished the toast with heaps of butter, talked endlessly on the telephone - and Don read the book on architecture.

Phoebe had a steady job: she worked part-time at the library. The little money she earned paid the telephone bill and bought food. She worked part-time at the main library in the Northern town, they had lots of books, but people used the library for the computers. At the library Phoebe stacked returned books. During her lunchbreak she would check her email and read a little, but working at the library, surrounded by so many books was changing her ideas about books. She could no longer hold long books and serious books she found hard to open. The smell of booze and cigarettes made her spiteful. A sleeping man with a closed book made her bump the trolley she was pushing into his chair and startle him, she emitted involuntary grunts when a romance novel was loaned out, she laughed when a spotty kid held Nietzsche ostentatiously. She would apologize and afterwards she did feel guilty, but at the time she wanted all of them to dissipate like the dream of London. Her boss was friendly, but when he spoke about the latest book to make a stir Phoebe had to hide her grimace behind a façade of niceness. The other girls were young and trendy and they talked of life as though life was one long summer night spent in a beer garden with music and smoke and laughter and cold beer. The young men who worked at the main library and wore tight jeans and designer glasses that matched their designer boredom, they said hello and goodbye, and the rest of the day they reduced Phoebe to just another boring book that needed culling.

Phoebe had published a novel, but it never sold, there had been no publicity, nobody cared, it could not be found in the library where she worked, or the local bookstore. K. the book was about the kaleidoscope, it was tedious and longwinded. Don had showed some interest, but Don was busy painting. Don's paintings were old-fashioned and provoked laughter and mockery. Don was good with his hands, but his paintings were as banal as Phoebe's writing.

There was a car in front of the flat. The car belonged to Phoebe. She had bought the car brand new when she had landed her first job, excitement and joy inspired her to buy the car. The car was now missing its engine and wheels. The children who lived next door used the car for fantastic journeys. Phoebe enjoyed seeing and hearing the flights of fancy, of hearing names of faraway cities being called out. Don painted the car as a chariot and the children as cherubs.

The shop on the corner of the street was open to eleven, but Phoebe forbid Don to go to the shop after dark, the shop was infested with drunken kids who smelt of fast food and cheap alcohol. Many cups of tea went without milk, and many bowls of cornflakes were eaten without sugar.

During the dark hours Don and Phoebe watched the television that was powered by one pound coins. They would have preferred to read in bed, but the television was rented to them by the landlord and each month a collector employed by the landlord emptied the box. The box was attached to the back of the television. The man counted the money and ticked his little black book. He never spoke to Don and Phoebe. If they were ever short the landlord would show up and ask nicely for the rest of the money.

"You need to watch more television," said the landlord.

"We watch too much television," said Phoebe.

Don recoiled.

"You're a donkeyhead," said the landlord. He looked at Don. "You like television don't you?"

"Yes" - Don looked at Phoebe - "well -"

"Well what. Television is good for you," said the landlord.

"Yes," said Don nodding his head. Don was reduced to a grub on the carpet.

Phoebe paid the landlord.

Phoebe found herself watching the lowest form of television; it was a compulsion that had sneaked up upon her. Each evening while Don cleaned the kitchen after tea Phoebe would sit on the couch, tuck her feet under her bottom, and watch a television show that delighted in showing the nadirs society had to offer. The show put on the television the damaged, the illiterate, and the unashamed. Phoebe in a mixture of hate, pity, and embarrassment watched the unfolding show, cringing, moaning, laughing. She watched the smooth presenter work up the fools to play up and make even bigger fools of themselves. Phoebe couldn't work out if the presenter was excellent at his job or the fools on the stage clueless about the camera's ability to broadcast all their actions, histories, secrets into the homes of strangers. Phoebe shaking her head, holding the pillow tightly, readying it to cover her eyes as a child will do when watching a horror movie, knew that she was doing something wrong, but like a junkie she could not stop, she had to have her fix. Don knowing what Phoebe was watching took his time in the kitchen washing the dirty plates, wiping down the counter tops, watering his flower and herbs. He listened to the radio and stared out of the kitchen window onto the back garden.

"I know, but what can you do," said Don.

The dog was too busy eating up the leftovers of a sorry cottage pie to reply.

"Cup of tea, Phoebe?" said Don.

"Please," said Phoebe.

Don boiled the kettle and listened to the news.

"It makes her feel good."

If money allowed Don and Phoebe on a Friday would buy drinks and have a curry. They would drink and scoff the curry as though the curry was something special and they would talk about moving to London. They had never been to London; they knew London through television programs, books, music, and the radio. London was a shining beacon on a hill. The hill was covered in verdant grass, the flowers bloomed, the trees full of fruit. London was at the end of a very dark tunnel and it coruscated. London was infinitesimal, but it glowed blindingly. Deep in drunkenness their plan of moving to London solidified. They had sold all their possessions, packed the rest up, jumped on the train, found a nice flat somewhere hip and trendy. Within a concrete plan they would talk excitedly until sleep. Moving from dream to dream the move to London would dissolve as the spices seeped from the opening and closing pores. In the morning the talk of London was as childish as sucking one's thumb.

"It sounded so good," said Phoebe.

Don nodded his head, he still longed for travel and adventure.

Not forgotten but under a patina of dust a tent and two sleeping bags accumulated to a mound by the door. Mildew and moss dappled the covering.

Don and Phoebe had been avid campers. When they could afford the train they went for long weekends into the countryside and camped out. They had three maybe four favorite spots where they liked to pitch their tent. Don could not build a fire without the aid of matches or a lighter, but he could cook with a single pot, and he enjoyed brewed tea over an open fire, and he never complained in the morning about the bright light of the sun or the lack of sleep, or that he smelt of fire and was in need of a shower. Don liked to be outside. Don as a child had been taken into the countryside often. It was his happiest memories. His passion for camping and hiking easily rubbed off on Phoebe. She was a product of concrete and towerblocks and belligerent voices of drunken, frustrated fathers, and beaten mothers, and so inevitably was fascinated with the moon and the stars.

When Don thought about camping he thought about his father. Don's father lived at Wilson's Heavenly Nursing Home. Three times a week Don took his father for a walk through the park. The park was a good size and next to the manicured grounds of Wilson's Heavenly Nursing Home. The walk for Don was a return to childhood, and he hoped it was the same for his father.

The park had many winding paths that got lost under canopies of trees.

The old man always started the journey with tears. It was as though the open space scared him. As they left the grounds of Wilson's Heavenly Nursing Home and entered the park with the many trees the old man would stop crying. The old man would stop crying and laugh as a child would at the sight of rabbits, squirrels, and butterflies.

They always walked on the same path, it was a circle and it brought them back to the grounds of Wilson's Heavenly Nursing Home.

During the first part of the journey the old man would ask Don the same question over and over again. The question hurt Don and he would always give the same answer.

"Am I crazy son?" the old man would ask and Don would say, "no."

They would walk along the path and after the questioning and the clearing of trees, the old man would start to cry again. Don would hand him a hankie and tell him that he was just having a bad day.

After the crying the old man would then attack Don verbally, in the nursing home the old man had picked up some colorful expletives.

Don could remember the old man only swearing once before going into the home. They were watching a football match. Don's father had shown some excitement. The away team scored and won the big game in the dying seconds. Don's father used the F word. Afterwards he denied using the F word and said he had emitted fudge.

They would walk for an hour, going round and round. The old man would stop abusing Don to smell a flower. After the bout of swearing Don's father would once again ask the question if he was mad and again Don would say no. Surrounded by trees a tranquility came over the old man. "Well?" asked the old man. "No," said Don. The old man removed his tears with the hankie Don always carried.

"Am I mad?" asked the old man.

"No," said Don.

He asked the question twenty more times and each time Don said no. For some unknown reason Don left the path they always walked and took a different path. The path sloped. The old man held on to Don. On the way down the path the old man kept up his abuse of Don. For most of the walk they were in darkness, the trees allowing no light to enter. Don was determined to reach the pool he had seen. He could hear ducks. He hoped the ducks would stop the abuse. The trees drew back and the sun illuminated the path. They leveled out and now could see the ducks. The pool of water was dappled with lambent flecks of golden sunlight.

"If somebody spoke to me that way I would knock out his teeth," that was their introduction.

Don's father showed his gums. The youths laughed. The old man said something and one of the youths called him a name. They moved off the bench they were sitting on and walked towards Don and his father. Don let go of his father. The old man shouted something and the youths stopped. Don had never seen his father so belligerent. The youths bobbed up and down. "He's crazy. He thinks those ducks are unicorns," said Don. The old man screamed at Don. The youths started to laugh. Don held his father and turned around. As they walked up the path they could hear the youths mocking them. Don wished his father was dead. He knew it was a terrible thought, it hurt to think it, and the thought reverberated and kept hurting. Phoebe's parents were dead. Her younger brother wanted nothing to do with her. He could still remember those nights when Phoebe scared him half to death with tales of vampires and werewolves. Now that he did not believe in vampires and werewolves he found Phoebe flighty and a bore. He had no time for Don. Phoebe's parents were the victims of the asbestos the Council had used in the tower block to save them from fire.

"My father is on the declivity," said Don.

"I know," said Phoebe. Phoebe no longer visited Wilson's Heavenly Nursing Home. The abuse was too much. She never complained about the feculent air that hid behind the disinfectant and cheap perfume. She never told Don that she feared inertia, stagnancy, and death.

Don and Phoebe had a friend that called them "Donnie"

and "Pheebs." Mark was deaf, sometimes when he got excited he would shout.

Phoebe communicated with Mark using sign language. Don spoke slowly as though he was speaking to a French person.

Mark liked to drink. He would have Don walk with him to the shop on the corner for booze and wine. Mark always paid, so Phoebe never complained.

Mark worked at the benefit office. He was a good friend, whenever Don had a question, Mark would help with an answer. "I need to get on sick," said Don. "Develop a limp," said Mark.

They decided to drink on the way home. They had been to the shop. Mark had been to a party at the benefit office and was drunk. Mark carried a bottle of wine for Phoebe; Don carried a twelve pack.

"Kate stuck her tongue down my throat," said Mark. He was shouting. Don with a can of beer to his mouth said something. Mark stopped. He finished his beer, threw away the can, and took another from the ten Don was carrying. "I was going to bring her back here. I couldn't take her to my house. Mother's been upset lately," said Mark. They never saw the pack of youths that attacked them. Don was pushed over. He dropped the cans of beer to save himself. Mark was punched in the face. A tooth flew across Don's face. The wine bottle hit the pavement and smashed. The youths groaned and attacked Mark incited by their disdain for waste. They punched and kicked him. He rolled up into a ball and took the beating. Don had been left in the middle of the road. Before the youths were aware of him he fled. He stumbled as he ran; he bumped into a parked car and cut his right shoulder. He could hear the youths shouting. But above the shouting:

"Don! Don!"

Phoebe helped Don into bed. She gathered up his bloodstained clothes and put them in the washer that they hired from the landlord. Don watched a centipede crawl up the wall. The washer to work needed a lot of onerous coaxing. Sometimes the machine stopped halfway through its task and steadfastly refused to work for nothing. Phoebe had to pay with sweat and profanity.

"The centipede," said Don.

"What?" said Phoebe.

The centipede was long, its coat was shiny and ferruginous, and the numerous legs were yellow.

Don was more paranoid and depressed than hurt. He worried that the youths had followed him home and were waiting for him to leave the flat. He constructed many reasons why the youths had attacked him. He thought up bizarre causes as to why they had attacked him. One such idea was that Phoebe was cheating on him with one of the youths and the youth was violent with jealousy.

He wanted to call Mark. To go around to Mark's house and explain why he had left him, but he couldn't, he had no words, no way to explain why he had jumped up and fled.

The cut on his shoulder derided him. The cut on his knee was a mouth that when he moved laughed and mocked him.

"Do you want to walk with me to the library?" said Phoebe.

"No," said Don.

Phoebe after finishing her cheese sandwich sat down at the office computer. She checked her email. A story had been rejected. This she did not mind, now it was a sport, it had nothing to do with literature, she said to herself that they would not be having fish for tea. Facetiously, the whole thing was analogous to fishing.

The second email told her that she had won the lottery.

Phoebe had won four things: Don, a bottle of champagne from the library, a scratchcard for forty pounds and a short story competition when she was twelve. She cursed the judges of the competition.

Phoebe mixed up history and philosophy and hurried home.

The postman delivered bad news. Don had been given an interview at the benefit office. The interview would either find Don a job or a place in a job seekers' club.

Don experienced an apoplexy and developed a limp.

Instead of phoning Mark, Don phoned the doctor's office.

Don entered the doctor's office on the limp. He sat down on a hard plastic chair; this did not help the limp.

The waiting room was full; there were a lot of sick people. Don knew all the sick and all the sick knew Don. He waited for an hour and read a magazine about healthy people with lots of money. He thought about the poor people and their sicknesses and he thought about the rich people in the magazine and their fancy cars, their helicopters, their mansions. Don read about the food the rich had cooked for them. The food was fresh, it was void of poisons, it never made them sick. The food looked much better than the art on the wall in the waiting room. His ticket told him he had a long time to contemplate the differences between the sick and the healthy, the food and the art.

"You sick as well?" asked a junkie. His knees were knocking. It was not a silly question.

The doctor was young and had expensive glasses. He smiled and asked Don to undress. Don undressed. The doctor was affable and asked about Don's day and Don took this cue to complain about the leg. Don found it very easy to complain. He could complain about everything, but he could not complain about his back, he had already seen the doctor about the back and the pain it caused him. The doctor examined the leg, the back again just to make sure it was not the back again, and the arms. Don produced a groan each time the doctor touched him.

"The limp is psychosomatic," said the Doctor.

"Psychosomatic?" said Don.

Don asked to be put on sick benefit. The doctor said no. The doctor could have given Don a sick note, but the doctor was making his last stand.

"See you in a month," said Don.

"Severe headaches?" said the Doctor.

Don nodded his head.

Limping home during a downpour Don's shoe slipped through dog excrement that had been left on the pavement. The limp was cured.

Loud knocking awoke Don. The last time somebody had knocked so loudly on the door resulted in Don spending two weeks in HM Prison Liverpool. He had refused to pay the Poll

Tax. The night before he had been out with Mark at the local pub, they were drunk; Don had mocked Mark for paying the Poll Tax. Walking home Don saw an owl, a fox, and a deer. At first he thought they were hallucinations, but when he startled them, and they vanished into the night he knew they were real. That night was imprinted as a beautiful moment. In the morning two policemen watched Don dress and then they placed him in the back of their car and took him to prison. Phoebe visited Don. She had bought a paperback book and some magazines for Don to read on his prison bed. The guards told her that she couldn't give them to Don. She took them home; she read the magazines on the train and the paperback at home in bed. During the first night in bed she moved in her sleep. She awoke believing she was falling out of bed. She had rolled over the ridge that separated her from Don and down into Don's spot.

The knocking grew louder. It became a continuous hammering. The dog shot behind the couch and defecated. Too excited Phoebe could only manage knocking; her fingers were tied in knots, she could not work the key.

Don opened the door. He almost vomited.

Phoebe ran into the front room. Don was sure the youths had chased her home.

Don needed seeing to and so while Don cleaned up after the dog, Phoebe told him about the lottery win.

Don couldn't understand Phoebe. She was talking too quickly. He thought she was drunk. He went into the kitchen and boiled the kettle. Phoebe followed him and still her words were coming out of her mouth muddled. Don made two cups of tea. He still feared that the youths were outside the flat and waiting for him. Phoebe took a sip of the hot tea and allowed her words to find spaces on their own. Don listened to Phoebe. She was excited about the lottery win. She said things like, "it could be a new start," and, "we could escape this rain-soaked misery." Don nodded and the love that he felt for Phoebe sprouted wings and flew. Don sighed. Phoebe not hearing the sigh continued talking about the lottery win and how all they had to do was collect the prize. Love may do a lot of things, but love cannot put money in the pocket, it cannot transport two middle-aged failures a thousand and some miles; love leaves the belly empty, it cannot fill the water bottle; it cannot make the sun shine.

"It sounds wonderful," said Don.

Don draped an arm over Phoebe. He placed a kiss upon her sweat-glistened brow. He untangled the arm and left Phoebe in the kitchen and went into the front room. He turned on the television and placed his shiny socks on the coffee table. Phoebe followed and sat down. Don saw the look in Phoebe's eyes and recoiled.

"We live in a world where anything can happen," said Phoebe.

This was true. Don and Phoebe had seen a lot of things happen lately that when they were children were just ideas. There was no need for video tape now, even music was no longer tangible; the television could show any movie you fancied.

Don nodded his head. He surreptitiously eyed the clock above the fireplace. A documentary was about to start. He helped Phoebe take off her coat. Phoebe threw the coat onto the carpet. The dog found a new bed.

"It is ours. Not rented. No landlords. Ours. Yours and mine," said Phoebe. Don smiled. "We are only here for a short number of years and we can't continue living like this," said Phoebe. The smile had dissolved. The blush that had dappled her cheeks had faded.

"We can't take the dog," said Don.

The dog was asleep; Phoebe wore thick, furry coats.

"No," said Phoebe.

It was Phoebe's idea to leave at the end of the month. They would leave before the television meter collector had made his call. She said they would open the box behind the television with a screwdriver and use the money in the box for food and transport. All money owing the landlord would not be paid. "We could never come back," said Don. Phoebe smiled and took Don by the shoulders and twirled him around. It was Don's idea to take the television to the pawn shop and sell it. Phoebe said they should try and sell everything. At the weekend they would take all they possessed down to the flea market and sell things that only a few days ago they would have ran into a burning house to save.

Don with Phoebe's help wrote Mark a long letter. In the letter Don tried to explain why he had chosen flight instead of fight. Don with the aid of Phoebe tried to articulate that that night was now the bottom of the well of self-hatred. That if Don ever wanted to know where his nadir was all he had to do was search for that memory.

Don without Phoebe's aid added a PS and under the PS

Don begged for forgiveness.

To save money Phoebe said she would post the letter on her way to work.

Don pleaded with Phoebe not to steal from the library. Phoebe agreed that stealing from the library would be a bad thing to do. Phoebe had to deal with people trying to steal from the library every day. People liked to steal movies and music, but not books; some stole the pictures out of books, but never the books.

"We are really going," said Phoebe.

Don nodded.

The room was small; it reminded Don of his first bedsit. It took him a night to realize that the bedsit was not the best place to live. The man next door hung himself. The policeman looked at Don and Don felt the pity.

The bed took him back to living at his parents' home. It was a bed that betrayed him, that told lies, that falsified.

Don's father pointed to the unsealed envelope on the bedside table. Without looking Don stuffed the envelope into his coat pocket. "Where is the gray?" asked the old man. Don looking at the teeth in the glass of water didn't hear. The teeth were covered in moss. "When I was a boy the rain and the ground were wet and stayed wet," said the old man.

The carpet was threadbare. The walls stained.

"Yes, father," said Don.

Out of the window Don could see a pub. The red bricks had been blanched. The pub had closed down. The beer was too expensive. It had lost out to supermarkets.

"It would rain all day and everything was gray," said the

old man.

The pub had been a very busy place, lively and jovial, and people met and had fun and made new friends. Don had been there once. A fight broke out, and a man smashed a bottle over the head of another man.

"Yes, father," said Don.

The old man was propped up in bed. He had had eggs for breakfast. There was coagulated egg yoke still on his chin. He needed shaving. The old man had to shave himself. Don was amazed that he still possessed two earlobes and his nose.

"Once we are settled in London I will sort something out, I promise," said Don. He hated lying to his father, but lying was better than wishing the old man dead.

"You'll be drowned down there," said the old man.

Don leaned over and removed the coagulated egg yoke.

"We can't go for a walk today I have to hurry home and see Phoebe. We are going to plan our route to London," said Don. The old man looked beyond Don. He was looking at the sky through the window. "When I was a kid the cold really was the cold not like now," said the old man. He sighed. "Yes, father," said Don. The old man looked at Don. His face was very still. "That money will do you no good down there," he said. Don nodded his head.

"I need the restroom," said Don.

In the bathroom there was a cord. If pulled a nurse would show up. Once Don pulled the cord thinking it was the light. He felt very silly when the nurse showed him the light switch. The nurse called on Don's father five times a day. The old man was helped into bed and helped out of bed. The nurse showed

Don a similar cord next to the bed that the old man was able to pull. The old man would be looked after. Don would only have to spend a month away. The old man had lost the concept of time. He couldn't tell the time, the names of days and months were lost to him, and the year didn't mean a thing. Don just had to stay away for a month. On his return the nurse would say, "you've been gone a month," and Don would answer, "London is very expensive," and, "I much prefer the North." The nurse would agree with a nod of the head.

Walking home Don counted the money. He wouldn't tell Phoebe just how much his father had given them. He thought about the paints, the paint brushes, the canvasses he could buy. He stooped and stuffed some of the money into his sock. He would hand Phoebe the rest of the money and then go into the bedroom and hide the money between two books. The money would be as safe as if it was in a bank. Don stuffed the envelope into his coat pocket and crossed the road.

A convertible sports car stopped suddenly, loudly, before killing Don.

The man driving the sports car stood up and took off his sunglasses. "I nearly killed you," said the man. "Look up. You are killing your children," said Don. This was true. The air was not the real air it was the air that had been expectorated out of the convertible sports car.

Don hurried, not so much from the man, but from fainting. Convertible sports cars kill. The man shouted something derogatory, but Don's heart was too busy beating and so he could not hear what the man had to say.

Hurrying, Don thought about Phoebe. It was an

incongruous thought, but there was a nexus. They had met at a poetry reading.

"To all you parents out there, you do not love your children, you cannot love your children, because if you did you would stop producing airplanes, ships, trains, trucks, cars, motorcycles, cigarettes, televisions, radios, plastic this and plastic that, rubber this and rubber that, teddy bears, booze, lipstick, pushup bras, …"

The crowd applauded Phoebe's interruption. One man with a long beard and a bald head asked her if she had a book he could buy, but she didn't, and she apologized to the man. She felt sorry for him, he had a lovely beard, but the bald head looked like a razed forest.

As she was leaving Don held the door open for her. It was that simple, he held the door open for her. They talked and decided to meet the next day.

"I think we should move in together," said Phoebe.

Don nodded his head.

Feeling confident now that he had money in his back pocket, Don stopped at the shop, and bought a pack of four beers and a bottle of wine. Walking home he opened a can. He sipped the beer as he walked past the spot where Mark had been beaten. Not a mark or blemish marked the spot.

"What you doing?" said Don.

Don dropped the cans and wine bottle. Nothing opened, nothing broke.

Phoebe was attacking the black box behind the television.

"Stop," said Don.

The dog started to dance.

Phoebe stabbed the black box with the screwdriver. It was the only tool they possessed.

"He'll kill us," said Don.

"Who?"

Don was wiggling with the worms and maggots in the back garden. He reeked of the canal, verdigris, rotten eggs, and carrion. He crawled up the wall with the centipede. He was trapped in the fly's web.

Phoebe again stabbed the black box with the screwdriver.

Don feared that the screwdriver would go through the black box and the television.

"The landlord!"

Phoebe had forgotten about the brutality of the landlord. Don was about to explain to her what the landlord would do to them when the dog found its voice. The bark was loud and fierce. Startled, Don and Phoebe turned and looked at the dog. The dog barked even louder.

"See," said Phoebe.

Phoebe stabbed the black box with the screwdriver, this time with more vigor. The dog was encouraging Phoebe to break the black box. There was now a great happiness in the bark. Don went over to Phoebe and instead of stopping her as he knew he should he took the screwdriver and started to attack the black box. The dog remembered it had a tail and wagged it. Phoebe came from behind and struck the screwdriver with a hardback copy of *The Ragged-Trousered Philanthropists*. A shower of coins scattered over the carpet.

Phoebe, Don and the dog howled.

They took the black box off the back of the television and

carried the television to the pawn shop.

Don got very drunk, threw up, was helped to bed, and he had a dream that he was being chased around an iceberg by the landlord and a gang of youths.

They had two days before they had to leave.

Phoebe's boss turned up in a white van and cleared the house of all the furniture. He even took Don's paintings. He handed Don a paltry sum, but now Don could say he had sold his art, something Van Gogh could never say.

"This is not true, just before his death Van Gogh sold many paintings, and was the talk of Paris," said Phoebe's boss.

Without the distraction of the television, without the radio, without books, Phoebe and Don talked. Phoebe was eager to hit the road. Don finally arrived at the point where he knew they were going south.

They took the dog downstairs to the man who lived underneath them. They didn't know his name, but they knew that he was lonely and was going bald. He had MS and carried a straw in his jacket breast pocket. He used the straw to draw Guinness to his mouth. The dog wagged its tail. He welcomed the dog into his apartment. Don and Phoebe said goodbye. They felt sad, but happy. The man thanked Don and Phoebe and took out his straw. Don and Phoebe had to decline the offer to go for a drink.

They drank water from a plastic bottle. They dined off paper plates and with their fingers.

Phoebe took control of the budget.

Their passports were close to expiring, but they calculated that they would be at the iceberg before the final date.

At the library they planned their route. They used the internet, and many books. Phoebe photocopied page after page, she made notes and calculated, and made a book that she would carry around in her rucksack.

They went to the store and bought dry food.

After packing Don and Phoebe stood at the window and watched the light wane. They watched people hurrying along the pavement and cars zipping past. Fear and joy came in waves. They held hands, squeezed when the fear became too much. They sighed and released the joy.

The rucksacks looked heavy; Don feared they would be too heavy.

They did something very foolish. They went into town and dined at a very expensive restaurant. They drank red wine. They ordered steak. The food was exquisite. They were lightheaded and wanted to sing and shout. The waiter played along with the game. He was young and obsequious. He received a good tip. They said their goodbyes. They tried to work out why they were acting with wild abandonment. They knew they were being foolish, that somewhere along the journey the money they were spending would be needed, but they could not help themselves.

They went to their favorite pub in town and listened to a duo sing sea shanties. Friends unaware of their intentions asked about the writing, painting, the library, Mark, benefit claims, the dog. They sat in the beer garden and basked in the hot night. Phoebe drank pints and smoked a cigarette. Don had two whiskeys and thought about his father. He hated lying to his father, but it was better than wishing the old man dead. In the darkness they joined the two sleeping bags. The moonlight was strong and they could hear the dog underneath them barking. They embraced as young lovers do.

Osagie worked on commission. He lived with his mother in Lagos. They lived in a bungalow. Osagie had an older brother that lived in the Bariga neighborhood, he had a lot of money, and in his truck was an AK-47 rifle. Aziz was the one that bought Osagie the computer. He set him up on the internet and taught him how to send out unsolicited bulk messages indiscriminately. The lottery was Osagie's idea. Aziz was shocked just how many gullible people replied to the email.

Phoebe never told Don that she sent money to a Doctor Goldie to receive her prize.

GOING UP

A bus took them out of town and they walked a mile in the heat to the motorway. They would hitchhike to London; spend a day and night in London. Don would send a postcard to his father, they would visit some of the free museums, spend some time in the parks. From London they would hitchhike to Dover. They would catch a ferry to Calais. In the paper there had been coupons which they had cut out. With the coupons the price of the ferry from Dover to Calais was a pound. From Calais they would hitchhike to Paris. This would be the only detour. In Paris they would visit the free museums, spend some time in the parks. After Paris it was Antarctica.

They stood on the side of the motorway and took turns holding out a thumb. It didn't take long for them to find their rucksacks worked as chairs. A bag of peeled carrots sustained them.

"Every time we see a dead car we cheer," said Phoebe.

"What?" said Don.

"It's a game. It's called the dead car game. It will be fun," said Phoebe.

Morning soon slipped into midday.

"I thought we would be in London by now," said Don. He

wasn't being facetious. He sighed.

"I can't believe all these cars are passing us by and not one has stopped," said Phoebe. It was her turn to stick her thumb into the air.

"We are doing something wrong," said Don. He thought about asking Phoebe to show some leg. He knew that some motorists and lorry drivers liked to see some leg on a miserable day. Phoebe had nice legs.

It started to rain. They could not escape the rain. The rain cleared.

In the rising fog they sat and watched the train of cars fly past them.

"I used to think I was some kind of Gypsy boy," sang Don. Phoebe smiled and stood up.

"Put your favorite hat on," said Phoebe.

A woman in a big car took them to the nearest service station. The cars were getting bigger but the roads were staying the same size. The car had trouble parking. At the service station they had a cup of tea. The woman told Phoebe that she only stopped because she wanted to find out about the hat. The woman said that she was going in the opposite direction but seeing the hat made her turn around. Phoebe thanked her. Don returned from the restroom and sipped his tea. The two women laughed seeing the hat.

By the side of the road Phoebe found a pair of discarded headphones. She picked them up as though she was unsure just what they were. Still slightly perplexed she walked over to the rubbish bin.

"Keep them. They are the new kind. They are very

expensive," said Don.

Phoebe wrapped the headphones around her hand and stuffed the ball into her rucksack.

A man in a small car said they would have to climb through the passenger window. He said the passenger door was broken. The offer to the next service station was too good to pass up. Phoebe climbed in first. Don had a vision of the car with Phoebe's legs sticking out of the opened window disappearing into the night. He felt very silly. Once Phoebe was safely in the back seat and the car was not in motion Don climbed through the open space.

"I think he was a pervert," said Phoebe.

The man had offered them a room in his mansion. The mansion was deep in the woods. He said he had many acres and that the mansion was far away from nosy neighbors. The man spent the whole journey laying out the architecture of the mansion. He talked elaborately about each room. After traipsing through each luxuriant Don and Phoebe could understand why the windows were broken in the small car.

They had the first of the cheese sandwiches that Phoebe had made that morning. The bread was unbuttered. Phoebe had used a number of plastic knives to cut the cheese. The cheese was too thick. Freed from the cling film the cheese had a chance to breathe. The sandwiches tasted and smelt of plastic. They sat on the edge of the motorway and had the cheese sandwiches.

A lorry driver said that he could take them to Hull. Don looked at Phoebe. The lorry driver told them that they would save money and time by sailing from Hull to Rotterdam. Don really wanted to go to London, but Phoebe knew that the lorry driver was right and so she nodded her head.

It was a quiet ride. Don had tried to engage the lorry driver in conversation. He asked a number of questions. Each question was met with a dead end. Phoebe wanted to say something to Don but instead stared at the car tops as they zipped by.

Phoebe cheered. The lorry driver looked at Don. It was a man thing.

The fight was over the price of the tickets. Don thought that he was fighting over London and a missed opportunity to see the city. Phoebe thought he wanted to pay for the buffet, they still had a number of cheese sandwiches, the food did sound good, but the buffet was expensive. They parted, calmed down, and came back together.

"We are here now and the boat will soon be here," said Phoebe.

They had two hours to waste. They sat facing each other, silent, each wanting to break the silence. Don watched Phoebe preen her fingernails. The act exasperated him. Finally, he attacked his thumbnail.

"Hungry?" asked Phoebe.

Don puzzled shook his head.

"They don't digest; they rot," said Phoebe.

Don expectorated the fragment of chewed nail.

The waiting room was empty, the lorry drivers stayed in their lorries. The rain tapped the windows. The sea was silent as was the television in the corner. The lady at the counter told them that an announcement would inform them of the departure time. The heaters hummed softly. They were sat directly under a warm jet of constant air. Phoebe nodded off, while Don watched the television.

Phoebe was the first to move. The heat was too much. Don moved, but did not follow Phoebe. He lay with his back to a machine that dispensed bottles of water. The soft buzz smoothed his headache. Phoebe lay across a row of chairs. Her eyes were closed and her hands laced together.

The cheese sandwiches were washed down with water. They took turns filling up their water bottle from the taps in the restrooms. Don was excited to sail upon the sea. When he was a little boy his father and mother took him to Dublin. He could feel the sea, but he could not see the sea. A heavy fog lay above the sea. The fog was thick and reached up to the sky. The swell of the sea made him sick. He vomited and his father and mother embarrassed dragged him away from the mess. He had forgotten about the vertiginousness and orange mess.

Phoebe had never been to sea, but she had read Conrad, Melville and London.

Phoebe slept while Don watched the television. Something was happening somewhere but Don had seen it all before.

The orange glow of the setting sun made Phoebe and Don go outside and look at the port. A fuliginous glow loomed and seeped dying sunlight. The blue of the terminal building and car park looked metallic in the waning sunlight.

The waiting room slowly filled up.

"And to think we never even got to see Hull," said Phoebe.

Don hoped for a stamp, but the lady just made sure the picture in the passport matched the face before her. She was full of yawns and nothing else.

The ferry left port.

Don and Phoebe sat in the buffet area, but could not go up to the buffet. They could see and smell the food. It smelt good. Don bit his nails surreptitiously and removed the splinters from the tip of his tongue with his fingers. Phoebe went to the bar and bought a drink. They shared the drink and watched the diners refilling their plates. The food was stretched out along one side of the dining room and was illuminated by very bright lights that kept the food warm. Phoebe hoped for the kind of seas that Conrad, Melville, and London had to deal with.

A swell upset Don.

Phoebe removed her boots and put her feet across Don's lap. He rubbed her feet, this stopped him attacking what was left of the nails - the tips were bleeding. Phoebe closed her eyes and even though the dining room was loud and bright she slept. Don stopped rubbing Phoebe's feet and allowed the roll of the sea to carry him off to sleep. He slept as though he had taken a handful of benzodiazepines.

When they awoke the dining room was full of sleepers. It was the middle or close to the middle of the night. The buffet had been cleared away. Don was disappointed. The air was still thick with the aromas. Phoebe could smell feet. They left the dining room and went out on to the deck. The sea was still. The warm air was a silk sheet that lapped gently upon their faces. The warmth of the air made the sea smell not so much of rotting fish but of the salt that Phoebe used in her bath.

They held the safety railing and looked at a waning gibbous

moon.

There was no talk of them leaving their home. They had no home.

"We are deracinated," said Phoebe.

Don was listening to the vexed gulls.

They went back into the dining room and closed their eyes. Sleep evaded them.

Don watching the first of the light over the sea was joined by a lorry driver. He was a big man, bald, but had a jovial face.

"It used to be the biggest port in the world," said the lorry driver.

They talked for half an hour. He agreed to take them to Amsterdam.

"The red light district is the mire smeared over a beautiful woman," said the lorry driver.

They agreed to meet after debarkation.

Don told Phoebe that he had got them a lift to Amsterdam. She seemed pleased. They went to the restrooms and freshened up.

The Netherlands was indeed flat and dissected with overflowing canals.

The lorry driver bought them breakfast. They had eggs, ham, bread, and Heineken. The lorry driver did most of the talking. He used the word concupiscence a lot. The lorry driver said he liked being on the road, but he missed his wife and children. He told them that if they were in Amsterdam next month they could meet up and he would take them to Istanbul. The only thing he complained about the whole time was the little boys that climbed all over his lorry and tried to hang on.

"I've seen three, there could have been more. Stopped and found them under the back wheels. The lorry's weight squeezed everything out of them. Terrible," he said. He sounded very sad.

He said at night he prayed to God. He worried about his children and concupiscence.

As the lorry pulled away they looked upon the Centraal railway station. They smiled and hugged. They were so happy, they kissed. The double aa in Centraal told them that they were on their journey. It was really happening.

Before they had time to exhale a youth asked if they wanted a room, if they needed any drugs, if they wanted to see a performance. He was the first of many to hand over an advertisement. Phoebe called them, "buzzing flies." They made Phoebe think of the city as a rotting carcass.

Even before her first inhalation she wanted to leave the city. Don talked her into staying a night.

Phoebe felt very sad, after walking some, she changed her mind, it was a beautiful city, her idea of the city had been inchoate, flavored by the unsavory, it had a huge sore that was hemorrhaging and attracted "buzzing flies."

They wandered in circles and Phoebe's feet throbbed. She knew what Don was looking for but she didn't complain.

Crossing Dam Square Don was knocked by a tram. His right ankle swelled.

They sat on the steps of an old church, watched the cyclists, and finished the last of the cheese sandwiches. Don did his best not to moan. He nibbled away at the cheese sandwich and cursed his luck and the tram driver.

Phoebe went into a bar named Bulldog to use the restroom. Don waited outside and watched the water flow rapidly. The banks of the canal were covered in flowers and nodes of verdant moss. A bald man with glasses stood next to Don. He leaned nonchalantly on the rail and joined Don looking down into water flowing through the canal. After many questions Don owned up to being a painter. The man beaming moved closer to Don, touched elbows.

"Only when a pornographic movie emulates Las Meninas will we get to see the ultimate pornographic movie," said Don's new friend.

Phoebe had heard. She looked at Don.

"Diego Velázquez," said Don to Phoebe.

Phoebe quiet, looked at Don's new friend.

"Only when a director endeavors to capture the brilliance of Diego Velázquez will the pornographic movie move out of the gutter."

Don asked if they could spend the night in a bed. Phoebe agreed. They found a Christian hostel. Phoebe and Don had to split up. Don was shown a large room full of bunk beds. He picked a bottom bunk and took off his boots. His ankle throbbed. Too tired to walk, in too much pain to clean himself, Don slept in his clothes.

Phoebe washed, brushed her teeth and spent part of the time in a deep conversation with a girl from Germany. They talked about books and philosophy. The girl was very pretty. They got on and said they should keep in touch.

During the night the bunk was disturbed. Don was

awoken by the weight of a man dispersing along the mattress above him. Soft moans were followed by a soft rocking. Don was confused. The bunk rocked back and forth and the soft moans grew louder. Don didn't know what to do; he placed the pillow over his head. The man finished and slept. In the morning as Don put on his boots he could feel the other men staring at him. Meekly he peered over the edge of the top bunk. He could hear the men whispering and he knew they were talking about him. The top bunk was empty.

"That's the second time we have veered off course and we will never do it again," said Don.

Phoebe agreed and continued to hector Don about his tour guide skills.

They arrived in Antwerpen.

After finding out the price of a hotel room also included two ladies sealed head to toe in rubber they slept in Antwerpen-Centraal railway station. A wooden bench ran around the waiting room. Don had somebody's feet pressed into the top of his head and his boots rested on Phoebe's hat. In the morning they had eggs and croissants. They had water instead of Heineken.

From Antwerp they got a ride to Brussels. It was another pervert. He talked and talked to Don but kept his eyes on Phoebe.

Phoebe bought a steel pen and told herself that if a man tried it on she would poke him in the eye. She told Don to buy a cheap bottle of wine. She told him to save the wine until they had reached Africa. "We have to celebrate," she said. If somebody started Don now had something to hit the man on the head with. She was happy now that they were tooled up.

They had to catch a bus out of Brussels. From the bus stop to E19 it was an hour walk.

On E19 they walked in single file towards the oncoming traffic. Don sang the same song over and over again. Don had not been blessed with a singer's voice, or the acumen to use his inner voice. Phoebe not being able to stand another rendition screamed at Don. The scream was dampened by the roar of traffic. Don got the message.

They spent two hours under a bridge drying off, resting their legs. The rain fell and cars hooted their horns.

"Why is it that the car reduces the person inside the car to an arsehole?" asked Don. "If we met one of these people on the street, in the library, in the pub, we would have a chat."

A lift dropped them off at a service station outside Mons.

Whoever should have been at the till was missing. So Phoebe and Don stole three sandwiches and a bottle of warm lemonade. They sat at the edge of the motorway and shared the sandwiches and bottle of warm lemonade. They felt guilty, but didn't share their guilt, it was easily superseded with joy as they chewed and washed down the mush with the warm lemonade.

They walked quietly, almost happy.

Phoebe had to urinate behind some bushes. Don sat down and rubbed the swollen ankle. A fancy car stopped. Don stood up and saw an attractive middle-aged woman draped in pearls sitting in the driver seat. Before Don could open his mouth the attractive middle-aged woman draped in pearls saw Phoebe hurrying to her rucksack and sped off. Don cursed his luck. "I could have met you one service down," he said. Phoebe just shook her head and pulled up her pants. Don felt foolish and shrugged his shoulders.

Squabbling they entered France.

They pitched the tent in a field. In the morning they were surrounded by cows. The sunlight was blinding; the stench unbearable. They hurriedly packed away the tent, and headed back to the motorway.

They continued to bicker. Phoebe complained that Don was walking too slowly and when they changed places Don complained that Phoebe was walking too fast.

A traveling toothpaste salesman told them that Boris Vian had invented the flavored toothpaste. They smiled and nodded their heads. He played loud jazz and told them about raspberry toothpaste. After dropping them off outside of Valenciennes he handed them two tubes of pineapple flavored toothpaste. As he drove off he shouted, "watch out for the eels!"

They spent the day and night in Valenciennes and slept in the Watteau train station. Don had a strange dream. He was on an island and the island was covered in wild vegetation, with tall trees and loud exotic birds. The island was floating above a blue sea that was shrouded in a soft mist. The mist as it ascended turned to rain. The rain fell gently. It tasted of pineapple.

The walk out of Valenciennes was onerous. They took off their coats and wrapped them around their heads, covering their necks. The tarmac was soft. It was as though they were walking through wet sand. The reek of oil in the air made them dizzy. The sky above them was iridescent. Their legs ached.

They fought nonstop and called each other names, inaudibly.

Don thought he had coughed up blood, but it was phlegm.

Phoebe wrapped a t-shirt around her face. Don used clean boxer shorts.

The motorway was very busy; a car or a truck had nowhere to stop.

They walked on, despondent, their heads down.

Don was the first to see the parked car. He shouted something and started to run. Phoebe followed. They ran as best they could. The car had been abandoned. Don removed his rucksack and sat down. He was red in the face and short on breath. Phoebe did the same. They sat with their backs to the car, looking out over a field that could have stretched all the way to the sea. They were exhausted. The only thing they had to eat was dried fruit. The car was dead. They had forgotten to cheer.

The water was warm.

Phoebe started to cry. Her bottom lip quivered and a single tear ran down her face. Don struggled and finally managed to place his arm around her shoulder. The weight was too much so Phoebe freed herself. They sat in silence. The only solace being the car blocked out the sun.

Phoebe swore loudly. The word was followed by a long scream. Don opened his eyes. Phoebe with the help of the parked car climbed to her feet. She helped Don up.

"Come on," said Phoebe.

Don smiled. Phoebe wiped away the dry river bed and smiled.

They picked up their rucksacks and started to walk.

A sports announcer in a flash black sports car said he was on his way to do the commentary on a football match. The flash black sports car looked very dangerous. The sports announcer did have a unique voice. Phoebe sat in the back seat. Don sat in the front and tried not to stare at the driver. The seats were leather and plush. The sports announcer handed out cold water and said that Paris wasn't far. He put the car into gear and they flew down the motorway. Don and Phoebe were very excited and never once thought of asking the sports announcer to slow down. The car reached one hundred and ten.

"I've had this baby doing one twenty," said the sports announcer. "I was on the M1. It was a sunny day, if you can believe it. It was perfect."

Outside of Paris they had a fine meal and the sports announcer paid. Don and Phoebe feigned an interest in sport. Phoebe was shocked just how much Don knew about football, cricket, snooker and darts. It turned out Don was quite the expert on darts.

Don and Phoebe changed seating.

Phoebe kept saying the word, "braggadocio." Don and the sports announcer were convinced that Phoebe was asking for a baguette.

They arrived in Paris in splendor.

The sports announcer turned up the music and they listened to The Beatles as they passed under an aeroplane landing. Phoebe recoiled thinking the aeroplane was about to hit the car, but the aeroplane passed them by and The Beatles were crystal clear and very loud. Phoebe sighed. The sports announcer liked The Beatles. He knew a lot of things about

The Beatles.

"That was the Charles de Gaulle Airport," said the sports announcer, showing his even white teeth.

Don consumed a chocolate bar as Paris opened up before him. The car, the sports announcer, Phoebe dissipated as he twisted his neck and greedily gobbled up the streets, the houses, the shops, the people. He felt giddy and silly. He had to keep still and keep his lips glued so as not to do something silly or say something ridiculous.

Phoebe and the sports announcer exchanged nods and smiles.

The sports announcer shook his gold and pointed out Paris. He knew a lot of things about Paris.

"I'll be there tonight," said the sports announcer, pointing to the Stade de France. "It's going to be a great match."

He took them on a tour of Paris, detouring many times. He talked nonstop and told them many interesting things. He pointed out many famous buildings and told a history for each famous building.

His road rage scared Don and Phoebe. And when he almost got into a fight with an ice-cream man Don and Phoebe thought about jumping out of the car and running away.

Finally, the sports announcer parked up by the Seine River, close to the Eiffel Tower, and opened the boot of his car without stepping out of the car.

"We should eat at Le Jules Verne Restaurant," said the sports announcer.

Before Don and Phoebe could nod their heads a phone rang.

The sport announcer handed Phoebe a few notes and his phone number. She felt very dirty.

For three nights Don and Phoebe slept at Charles de Gaulle Airport. They traveled by the Métro.

Don nearly fought with a waiter in the Latin Quarter.

"You have a casserole?"

"You just call me an asshole?"

The waiter was an American student.

Phoebe bought a book from the Shakespeare and Company; it was Proust in French. Phoebe could not read French.

They visited Oscar Wilde and Modigliani. They got lost and fought. Phoebe had to sit down near Arthur Rimbaud and complained about her throbbing feet. It was a new and strange sensation.

The crowds around Philippe Auguste were too much so they walked. It started to rain.

It was a sad night. A group of Africans were flying home to Cameroon. Don and Phoebe watched the men and women hand over their tickets. The next day they would be in Yaoundé.

They spent most of the day on the Métro, trying to get out of Paris and reach the A10. It was humid. The Métro was overcrowded. A young girl stood up, started speaking, told a long story, and then begged. It broke Phoebe's heart to ignore her. The young girl was dirty and must have been around twelve. She was barefooted and had a little mustache.

After the Métro they caught a bus that dropped them off two miles from a good hitchhiking spot. The walk was hard. The humidity lay heavily upon them, pushing them down, mocking them.

"We should have bypassed Paris," said Phoebe.

They had spent too much money and energy.

At the side of the motorway, under a canopy of Kudzu, they watched a thunderstorm in the distance. The clouds were a black soup, the lightning blinding, and the thunder deafening.

The storm passed over Paris.

Cars and trucks passed by but none stopped so Don and Phoebe slept in their sleeping bags under the canopy of Kudzu.

Phoebe counted the money and said they were running low. Don said that they should try to get to Morocco as quickly as possible.

"I think it is something like eight miles from Spain to Morocco," said Don.

Phoebe opened up her book and found Algeciras.

"The price is good and it only takes thirty-five minutes," said Phoebe.

Phoebe closed the book. Don found a piece of cardboard and wrote Madrid in bold letters.

A car stopped and offered to take them to Tours.

After Tours Phoebe refused to talk to Don, they had fought over something trivial, and Don had said something mean. Something very mean, something on a par with wanting a father dead. He couldn't remember what he had said. He was in front, and he could feel Phoebe breathing down his neck. His ankle throbbed. He tried to remember, but he couldn't. Phoebe was red in the face and blowing.

A British lorry driver took them to Bordeaux. He was talkative. He talked about the weather and laughed loudly at his own jokes.

They walked through Bordeaux without stopping.

Outside of Bordeaux they sneaked onto a campsite that was surrounded with vines.

"I am going to write a poem," said Phoebe.

The last poem Phoebe had composed was ten years back when they were living with Peter and Roger.

"I am going to call it Popping Blisters in Bordeaux," said Phoebe.

Don with a hot needle popped Phoebe's blisters.

They overslept and were caught. Phoebe paid the rent as Don dismantled the tent. At a shop they bought bread and one banana.

Phoebe hobbled and had to stop when the pain got too much. Phoebe's feet were cursed by Phoebe and Don. Phoebe could feel the pus soaking her socks.

Don carried Phoebe's rucksack until they found a good spot to hitchhike. They had to refuse two lifts because the ride would have dropped them off in the middle of nowhere.

They crossed into Spain under more rain and lightning.

A young man picked them up. He kept the windows down and said something about air-conditioning. The young man's driving scared Don and Phoebe. As the car careened along the road Don and Phoebe opened their mouths and received a mouthful of bugs. Spitting out legs they watched the landscape blur. The young man laughing loudly blew his horn when they came across roadkill.

"¡Despierta!"

Don and Phoebe were confused but after the tenth time

they joined in.

"¡Despierta!"

The young man smoked and when he was not talking on the telephone turned and tried to get Don to smoke.

"Los hombres ya no se despierta!"

The car sped through the snow. They watched in amazement the snow zipping past. The car almost lost the road, Phoebe screamed, Don swallowed a mouthful of bugs, and the young man laughed loudly.

The young man finally stopped the car and they climbed out. They could see Pamplona through the falling snow.

They had food at a roadside diner. The young man tried to explain that he was going to Pamplona to run with the bulls.

After eating they jumped back into the car, the young man took them around Pamplona and dropped them off at a good place to hitchhike from.

The grass was brittle and turned to dust upon touch. Phoebe closed her eyes while Don watched the road. The cars were all going in the opposite direction. Don spent his time removing insect legs from between his teeth.

"Do you remember the time when Peter and Roger thought you said you loved a good double entry when you said you liked a good double entendre," said Phoebe. She laughed mockingly. This hurt Don and Phoebe knew. It was like sticking needles into his eyes.

"I thought it was you," said Don.

"No it was you," said Phoebe.

"I thought we were going to get into an accident in that car," said Don.

"I thought he was asking me to make you into a cuckold, the way he made the horns with his hands. He was rather good looking," said Phoebe.

Don grunted.

They saw very little of Madrid.

A young French couple took them down to Algeciras. They stopped just before Algeciras, smoked some marijuana, and watched the sea undulate.

The young French couple were much in love and kept kissing and touching each other. The boy had dreadlocks, the girl covered in tattoos. The girl spoke very good English.

"I hope those tattoos stay the way they are now and don't smudge as the skin on her arms sags," said Don.

The radio played Bob Marley as they boarded the ferry. The young French couple paid for the car. Don and Phoebe sat in the back, silent.

Don and Phoebe kissed with wild abandonment. The French couple laughed and went to the bar to buy drinks. Don and Phoebe, bathed in sunlight, hugged, laughed and danced. The sea air made them lightheaded. They giggled and leaned over the safety railings. Looking down they thought they saw whales, dolphins, seahorses and mermaids. Their eyes danced over the froth of the sea. They listened to the mellifluous music the sea produced. It was a sea dappled with lambent flecks of golden sunlight. They had never been so happy. They waved goodbye to the Rock of Gibraltar as though the Rock of Gibraltar was an old man standing at a back door. Africa was a dazzling interlude between the sea and the sky, iridescent, magical. The word Tangier thrilled them.

They were forced to sit down. They picked up their drinks and toasted the young French couple who were smirking with bewilderment. They smoked more marijuana.

"Tangier," said Don and Phoebe and they laughed loudly.

"Pillars of Hercules," said the young French girl.

The Strait of Gibraltar was calm.

Tangier coruscated.

Don and Phoebe hugged and kissed the young French couple.

"We've done it," said Phoebe. "We've really done it."

"I love you," said Don.

"I love you back," said Phoebe.

The ferry slowly entered Tangier.

Before having their passports stamped the young French couple said goodbye.

Don and Phoebe saw the young French couple after having the passports stamped sitting on white rocks overlooking the sea and cranes.

Don and Phoebe walked through the port gates and into Tangier in a dreamlike state. The sunlight, the white walls, the dusty streets were blinding. The real spread slowly over the unreal as Don and Phoebe became aware of where they were. Phoebe's head was full of the Zulu, the Fuzzy-Wuzzy, and Conrad's Skeletons. Don's head was full of elephants, giraffes, and lions.

They followed the traffic, giddy with disequilibrium.

Incoherent, they conversed, non sequiturs piling up crazily, unrealistically, joyously about the rest of the journey.

They looked at the gates, tall and ochre, two arches where

traffic poured through the orifices, and tried to read the Arabic writing upon the walls. They were being puerile, but knew, and laughed at the fatuousness. Two red flags fluttered. The sky was cerulean and without clouds. The sun had never seemed so unblemished. The light was heavy and a burden on the eyes.

Under a sign for motorists Phoebe counted their money. She complained about how much they had spent. Don removed his rucksack, leaned against a wall, and searched for the bottle of wine.

Don removed his rucksack, leaned against a wall, and searched for the bottle of wine. He wanted to celebrate.

The flow of traffic was unrelenting. Tourists waved. The air was heavy with celebration. Don was desiccated. He found the wine bottle. He was beaming.

Don sat down and dangled his boots into the dusty road.

A car zipped past and ran over Don's boot. He howled loudly and dropped quickly to the pavement. Phoebe helped him remove the boot. The sock was shiny and reeked. Phoebe reluctantly peeled the sock away from the foot. The money he had hid down the sock bloomed in the sunlight.

"You bastard!" said Phoebe.

Don was tongue-tied.

Phoebe plucked the wad of money and held it up. She counted it quickly and added it to the other bundle.

Don blew futilely on the throbbing foot.

Phoebe helped put on a clean sock. Sand between his toes chafed. Don tied his bootlaces gingerly and afterwards picked up his rucksack. Phoebe wanted to scream at him. He knew that Phoebe wanted to scream at him, so he kept his head down and limped after her. Phoebe hurried.

Youssef had a peculiar laugh but this could have been the result of Phoebe's explanation of why they were hitchhiking. He said he didn't want their money, but he wanted something. Phoebe offered him the pen but Youssef said he had a thousand pens. Looking into her rucksack Youssef produced the copy of Proust. He was very happy.

Youssef was small, had large ears, and a massive smile. He drove a white van and chainsmoked. Don climbed into the back and made a throne out of heavy small wooden boxes. Phoebe sat in the front. Youssef was Tunisian and he was going to Rabat.

"Do not travel down the middle of Africa. Africa is not Europe. Go to Accra, Ghana and find a fishing boat that will take you to Libreville, Gabon. The world is not flat my friends. The world is a ball, it is round," said Youssef.

Phoebe wrote down the names. She turned and looked at Don. Bouncing up and down upon his throne Don tried to shrug his shoulders.

"Upon the Gulf of Guinea you will glean many things," said Youssef.

"Yes I believe we will," said Phoebe.

Youssef lit a cigarette and turned up the radio.

Phoebe looked out of the window at the verdant landscape. She was sad that she hadn't had the opportunity to explore Tangier. She promised herself that she would return.

"Roads are the same all over the world," said Youssef.

Phoebe nodded her head.

"You look beyond the road at something and you see something beautiful, but you must ask yourself is it really real or just your imagination filling in the blanks that boredom has created," said Youssef.

"I always thought no two roads are alike, but here now, traveling along this road the only thing I can say is yes, I am in agreement with you, but last week I would have disagreed with you most vehemently," said Phoebe.

Youssef laughed and shook his head.

"Remember the sea is a whore and she will take any paying customer," said Youssef.

Phoebe blushed.

Don banged his head as the van passed over a number of holes in the road. Don was sure that Youssef was aiming for the holes intentionally.

They had lamb and a Flag Speciale in Youssef's favorite bar in Rabat. The bar was small. Don played with the dirhams as though the money was a toy. After the meal they said goodbye to Youssef. He gave them lots of advice, too much to comprehend, too much to store away.

They spent three days in Rabat. They hung out around the Medina, sat outside a bar and sipped on a bottle of Flag Speciale; they bought corn from vendors who grilled the corn on open coals. Don and Phoebe loved the charcoal taste.

On Rue des Consuls they found a good restaurant that served wonderful sandwiches. Don could not take his eyes off the rotating, bubbling meat. He had lost ten pound.

They slept in Rabat's bus station. They spent most of the day on the rocks. They were told that Rabat once had a very beautiful beach.

They fought over McDonald's for breakfast. Phoebe was steadfast.

"You voted for her," said Don. "So don't act all pure." This was a sharp knife into Phoebe's heart. Don always played this card when they were at their nadir. It was Phoebe's cross to bear.

They spent a couple of dirhams on bread and pastries for the road.

They caught a bus.

They walked in silence.

The whole day they refused to talk. Phoebe used her eyes, a feigned smile, her hands; Don grunted.

They spent the night in the tent overlooking the sea. In the morning they saw two buildings standing in the water.

Ahmed was not very talkative. He was transporting computers to Bamako, Mali. The only thing he asked for was that they talk nonstop. The radio was broken.

Ahmed was a cautious driver.

Phoebe felt as though she was training a parrot. Ahmed picked up the words easily, the sentences flowed, but he found it hard to comprehend the meaning of so many superfluous words.

The inside of the truck reeked of sweat and tobacco. Don and Phoebe were squeezed into one seat. The rucksacks were with the computers, which were broken into worthless pieces. For the first day they sat ridged and dug elbows into each other's ribs. The second day they relaxed and allowed their malleable bodies to find a comfortable place.

"I hate sand. My inner thighs are red raw," said Don.

"The same here," said Phoebe.

Nodes of verdant grass had appeared incongruously.

They slept close to the truck in the tent while Ahmed slept in the truck. They dined together, and when Ahmed prayed they would go to the back of the truck. They didn't discuss the landscape or the insects that bit them. They never inspected the flowers and trees. What locals they came across they tried to interact with but only received a confused smile.

Ahmed didn't use maps and he never spoke about the road.

"All this used to be desert," said Ahmed. He was sad.

Black rock spouted out of verdant seas of grass and weeds.

Under a full moon, under a blanket of glistening stars, to the cacophony of insects Don and Phoebe contemplated their journey. A fear swelled within them. Suddenly, they were aware of how precarious and lonely they were. They held hands.

Fear worked as a strange glue.

With the aid of a cracked mirror Don trimmed his beard. The bathroom was small; the green tiles had probably been white. The water from the shower head cascaded lackadaisically. The toilet groaned. They had found a cheap room in a hotel in the Zone.

The days were humid, blindingly bright; the nights filled with continuous thunder, lightning, and heavy rain. If it rained during the day the drops of rain evaporated on touch.

They lived on street food, fish and toh. They had gumbo which they ate with their hands.

The Niger River had spilled over and many streets had been abandoned.

"I don't believe it," said Don.

Phoebe was staring out of the window. Slowly she was acclimatizing to the incongruities. Bamako was like any other growing, living, breathing city. A patina of pollution hung over the city, the cacophony of the streets filled the dome, and people were hurrying from and to work.

"What's up?" asked Phoebe.

"Look at my nails," said Don. He held up the back of his hands, his fingers splayed.

Phoebe nodded. She was proud, but she couldn't let Don know how proud. She didn't know why she couldn't let Don know how proud she was of him. She felt sad and angry at herself.

Don sat on the bed and preened the long nails.

"I am cured. No longer do they hurt. Look they're no longer red raw," said Don.

They spent a week in the Zone.

On the outskirts of Bamako they spent the whole day and night beside a very busy road.

The next day they tried to walk to RN7. Finally a lift got them onto the road.

Three lifts got them out of Mali and into Burkina Faso.

In Ouahigouya they met BadBoy. He smoked big fat cigars, which he crushed with his gold teeth. He wore a baseball cap, and he was in need of a belt. He was very, very tall, and thin, and his gait comical.

There was an air of menace about BadBoy, but he seemed to like Don and Phoebe. He towered over them, and slapped Don on the back which hurt.

BadBoy treated them to rice with sauce and spaghetti. He flirted with the women that cooked the food. He tipped well and received the coquettish light kisses with a loud laugh that showed off his gold teeth. He called each and every woman that he passed, "mother."

They washed the food down with milk. It was a treasured meal.

BadBoy was talkative and very funny. He called Don, "Donnieboy," and Phoebe, "Phebbygirl."

BadBoy had a stare that scared away the begging children and feral dogs.

"Oil Oil Baby!" he sang all the time and then he would slap "Donnieboy" on the back.

The Land Rover was white and new. Phoebe climbed into the back. Next to her they stored the rucksacks. BadBoy said he had something in the trunk. They nodded their heads. They never asked about what was in the trunk. Don feared drugs; Phoebe hoped not a dead body. They were just happy that BadBoy had promised a lift all the way to Accra, Ghana.

Both independently had the feeling that they could end up in a ditch somewhere, but they didn't share this faint hint of fear.

"Oil Oil Baby!"

BadBoy paid little time looking what was ahead. The Land Rover careened off the road many times. Twice it almost rolled over. It was a white knuckle ride. He didn't stop for pedestrians or cattle. When a big bug splattered against the windscreen BadBoy sang loudly: "Oil Oil Baby!" No longer able to slap Don on the back he punched "Donnieboy" on the arm. The gold rings cut into the skin. Don wincing, smiled, and nodded his head.

BadBoy practiced his marksmanship with his thumb and fingers. His imaginary gun fired rockets. He shot at things indiscriminately. With a smile and a wink he had "Donnieboy" practicing his aim as well.

"Oi! Oi! Baby!"

As the Land Rover made ease of the croaked road the landscape blurred into untranslatable images, trees became trains, the sky and the land merged.

Phoebe did her best not to let the rap music entice her to vomit. Of all the people it was Elvis that saved her the embarrassment of making a mess of the inside of the Land Rover. BadBoy was a huge fan of 70s Elvis. He turned the volume down and sang along with his eyes closed.

"Donnieboy" was told to watch the road for "mothers." Cattle or men should not disturb the music.

"Do you know what the best thing the white man introduced to Africa is?" asked BadBoy.

Don and Phoebe shrugged their shoulders.

"The credit card!" said BadBoy. "It's a lot easier to carry around in your pocket."

"Compared to what?" asked Phoebe.

"Goats! Phebbygirl," BadBoy laughed and he shot wildly with his imaginary gun at the sinking sun. He blew away the imaginary smoke and exchanged a look in the mirror with "Phebbygirl." His eyes were orbs lambent with ivory.

At a gas station Don and Phoebe cleaned up while BadBoy filled up the tank. Phoebe offered some money but BadBoy laughed and waved away the paltry sum. He bought them food and Coca-Cola. They thanked him profusely as he covered the gas station in dust.

During the night BadBoy forgot his mantra and the ritual of punching Don.

The Land Rover slowed to a pace and the radio was silent. Finally sleep overcame BadBoy.

They slept in their seats. After four hours they hit the road again. They stopped at Wa and had sao which they dipped into okra soup. Again BadBoy paid. Whenever Phoebe offered money BadBoy would get agitated.

"I am the man I am BadBoy and you are Phebbygirl," said BadBoy and his gold teeth and ivory orbs glowed.

BadBoy's exuberance obscured the vistas and his cigars overwhelmed the aromas and the taste in the air.

"You make me happy," said BadBoy.

"Why?" asked Phoebe.

"You've traveled a great distance and been in the presence of greatest and the only things you think about are sleep and food," said BadBoy. He sounded troubled. Sleep weighed heavily on his face.

"Food first," said Don.

BadBoy tutted loudly and shook his head.

Don and Phoebe exchanged a puzzled look.

"You would have been better off with a pocket full of goats instead of that paper money in your pocket," said BadBoy.

The Land Rover suddenly sped off the road. BadBoy with his face almost pressed up to the windscreen watched carefully as the beams of light cut through the darkness. Don and

Phoebe were confused and the fear rose as the car careened wildly through the darkness. They could see nothing. They tried, but could not get through to BadBoy.

BadBoy obsessively drove on and on. Every now and again the car was shocked by a rock.

Minutes became hours. The darkness waned. Silhouettes stood out from the darkness. The silhouettes could have been many cathedrals.

Finally BadBoy stopped the car.

"I think we are back in Mali," said Don. He was unsure. He looked at Phoebe for help, but she was as confused and just as helpless.

They were vertiginous with fear. They were nowhere, surrounded by the dessert, and rocks, and desolation. Even the sky looked incongruous.

BadBoy was not the same BadBoy that had called them "Donnieboy," and "Phebbygirl." He was rigid, and hardly looked at them. The ivory in his eyes was dull.

BadBoy got out of the Land Rover.

Don and Phoebe didn't know what to do.

Don was startled by the knocking on his window.

Don and Phoebe got out of the car. They were surrounded by rock draped in the last of the night. It was as though they were trapped at the bottom of a rock caldron. They could not escape. Don was close to vomiting. Phoebe gripped her pen and prayed.

BadBoy was silent and serious. The vim had gone. He was no longer the clown. Don and Phoebe didn't know what to expect.

The rock was a dark brown.

It was cold. Don felt febrile, he shivered uncontrollably. Phoebe had her fingers on the pen in her pocket.

They followed BadBoy.

The path rose steadily. They stumbled, struggled, used their hands.

Don started to cough. He was retching.

By the time they had reached the top of the path the rocks were ferruginous and foreign. They looked soft and porous.

BadBoy stopped at the foot of a cave. The rictus was as welcoming as any mouth.

Don and Phoebe could not help but show their fear. Don wanted to cry. Phoebe gripped the pen tightly and the pen snapped. Ink ran down her leg.

BadBoy started to laugh. He entered the cave and his laugh echoed loudly. Don and Phoebe overcame their pusillanimity and entered the cave.

A flame startled them.

BadBoy was sat down.

"Come here," said BadBoy. His voice was imperious.

They walked to the flame.

"Up there," said BadBoy.

Don and Phoebe looked up. BadBoy produced more fire and the flames illuminated more of the cave.

Don and Phoebe could not believe their eyes.

The roof of the cave was covered in a celebration of life.

"As old as man himself," said BadBoy.

A deep sigh of wonder turned into laughter of complete and utter joy.

Accra forced them to exhale.

The hotel room was more than Phoebe wanted to pay, but it had a good view of the sea. The hotel was on Quarmine Road. It was small, but nicely furnished. The concierge was affable and full of advice. William was old and kept repeating old jeremiads.

As Don searched for a captain to take them across the Gulf of Guinea, Phoebe worked as a maid at the hotel. William, except for the old jeremiads and the fears of seeing more aceldamas, was a good boss. He liked Phoebe and her silly smile.

After tea, as the sun was setting, they would climb upon an abandoned building and bathe in the warm water.

They spent a month living, slipping with ease into city living. They had never lived in a city as big as Accra. They went for long walks, used the monorail. They went to bars and restaurants, and one evening even went to the theater and listened to the National Symphony Orchestra Ghana do a tour of the world. They went to the National Museum, and visited Kwame Nkrumah Memorial Park.

One night in The Havana a drunk told Don and Phoebe they would have better luck in Cape Coast. Don bought the drunk a bottle of Star. The drunk thanked him with a nod of the head.

The next day Don and Phoebe caught a bus to Cape Coast.

They spent a day at Cape Coast Castle. The newly whitewashed walls were green. Moss hung from the cannons that faced the sea. Drops of seawater dripped from the moss.

They walked along the cannons and looked out at the sea.

The waves battered the castle's walls.

At the vegetable market they bought tomatoes from a woman who had the tomatoes built up into a pyramid and was balancing the pyramid on the top of her head.

An old woman crouched before a mountain of okra told them they would find a captain in Elmina.

They traveled by TroTro.

The bus dropped them off by the sea.

Elmina was a hive of activity.

Don and Phoebe wandered along the rocks searching for the perfect fishing boat. The rocks were home to many long narrow fishing boats that were lined up jostling for space. It was very busy, the fishermen were working hard; women were carrying loads upon their heads, and children sat on the rocks or swam in the murky waters.

As the water receded after washing the rocks, a stone walkway was revealed.

Don and Phoebe sat on the rocks and watched a number of men push a fishing boat out of the water. They breathed in the belches of the sea.

Palm trees spouted from pools of abandoned seawater.

Emilo was very tall with wide shoulders, his features were chiseled, the moustache bushy. Phoebe was smitten. Emilo was a Bubi and very proud.

He took them to a bar where fisherman silently played dominoes. Waves beat the outside walls of the dilapidated bar.

They entered the ruin and sat down in a corner.

Phoebe sat as close to Emilo as she could. Her eyes picked out each infinitesimal beauty spot that made up his muscular body, something she had not done as she traveled over the vast lands. To show that he wasn't inept, Don went to the bar and bought a round of drinks.

The bartender was rachitic and slowly removed the bottles from the fridge that hummed to the sound of the waves beating the sides of the bar.

The tolling of the beer bottles warned Phoebe to avert her eyes.

Emilo said he would take them on; they would get free board, free fish to eat, and very little pay. They agreed. Don went back to the bar. The hypnagogic bartender struggled but finally found three more bottles.

"We set sail tomorrow," said Emilo.

Their bottles met loudly over the slanting table.

"Last orders," said the bartender. "Sorry."

Don feared the bartender had narcolepsy. To make sure he went to the bar and ordered three more beers.

"The sea is a beautiful lady and she loves man. But man has given her VD and so now the beautiful lady is very upset with man," said Emilo.

They emptied the beer bottles.

In the restroom, a man standing next to Don caught his eye. The man was laughing. His eyes were enlarged, sweat glistened in the waning sunlight, and foam had hardened in the corners of his mouth. Both men were very drunk. Don smiled fatuously.

"Emilo's fishing boat is as seaworthy as this bar but the sea is a whore and will take any paying customer," said the drunken man.

The first couple of days they lay on their backs, stared up at the sky, and did their best not to vomit. The sea was violent and showed no mercy to the fishing boat.

The canopy over the engine and steering was ineffectual. The rain fell slanted. It was Phoebe's berth. Emilo and Don slept in the front of the fishing boat. Don slept in the bow where he had to fold up his legs.

Emilo showed them the cleats and the ropes. He showed them how to open a beer bottle and how to light a cigarette in the wind. He pointed to where the sea and sky merge and showed them North, South, East, and West. He kept them far away from the engine.

Phoebe was First Mate. Don was crestfallen, but took it on the chin.

Emilo spent days showing them how to do knots, how to cast the net, how to pull in the net, how to separate the worthless from the good. He drank and abused them like any pirate captain would his crew.

"Work is good for the soul and we have two soles so we must work double hard," said Emilo.

Don and Phoebe worked hard. Emilo abused them for not working hard enough for his liking. Emilo liked to see sweat and strain. He abused Don and Phoebe night and day. The abuse was full of witticisms and wild abandonment of language; it was full of color and spice. They enjoyed the abuse, there was lots of abuse. They talked of staying with Emilo for good. The hands bled. The muscles screamed. Retinas were rearranged. Ears and sea coalesced as sea and seashells. They were no longer impenetrable, no longer opaque.

"The sea always provides. The sea is God's gift to man," Emilo said one starry night, he was very drunk. He showed off his tattoos and offered to fight them both. "Love the sea, treat the sea with love, and the sea like a loving wife will produce babies lots and lots of beautiful babies."

Off the coast of Annobón, they watched a tornado land and enter the island. It had been a clear day, hot and humid. The sea had been calm. The lapping water against the fishing boat was the jeremiad. The slapping grew louder. The sea lifted up the fishing boat as black clouds appeared overhead. Phoebe thought she could almost touch the clouds. The clouds swirled as though they were being stirred by a magical spoon.

A snake's head appeared out of the thick soup. It struck the sea.

Don and Phoebe feared the fishing boat was about to capsize. Emilo fought the sea with every inch of his body.

Emilo prayed loudly for the people of Annobón.

"The sea does not drown man; man drowns in the sea," said Emilo.

The peacefulness after the storm was a lover lying upon a warm bed seeing happiness spread over the vast topography of the loved one.

They sailed around Annobón and São Tomé and they caught many fish that they froze in an old ice box that once belonged to a bar.

A tourist boat from Ilhéu das Rolas sailed past and the tourists waved.

"What I wouldn't give for a cold pint of Boddingtons and some chips and peas," said Don picking flakes of fish meat from a bone. Emilo cooked the fish over a small fire that he made in the middle of the fishing boat. He used the bonnet of a small car to stop the fire from burning a hole in the hull.

"The sea is the only lover we have," said Emilo. Somehow he still had beer. He steered the fishing boat, sipped his beer and smoked a cigarette. "Once she has rejected us it's a eunuch's life for us."

They circled Bioko many times before docking in the Port of Malabo.

"The sea is rising because of the tears shed by the Bubi," said Emilo.

Bioko was a contracting and expanding paradise.

The port was crowded. Emilo nodded his head, held up his hands, and laughed with many locals. Emilo was very popular. Don and Phoebe watched him converse as they tried to pull themselves back from disintegration.

They sold the fish they had caught and left the fishing boat. They climbed into Emilo's battered car, they could see the engine.

They were sad that they were on the road again.

Emilo dropped them off at the Mercado Central and he went off to do some business.

They went and had a drink and something to eat and Emilo picked them back up after an hour.

They drove through an abundance of beauty. They saw Pico Basilé.

"You never see this on the telly," said Don.

Emilo lived in Riaba with a wife and three boys. Emilo's wife made fried plantain and chicken, topped with picante and mayonnaise. The boys looked at Don and Phoebe as though they had fallen off the moon and their father had plucked them out of the sea.

The children hid behind their mother and she tried to shoo them as she would with busy flies. Don and Phoebe tried to communicate with the children but were helpless.

Emilo drank beer and when he was drunk he scattered the children and kissed his wife.

Don and Phoebe pitched their tent and slept in the garden. In the morning they went back to the fishing boat.

Once they were back on the sea, Emilo told very dirty jokes that always ended in him exploding. He had more stories to tell than Scheherazade. They worked even harder and caught more fish. They enjoyed their time, the pain was pleasurable, and they felt the sea accepting them. The rope no longer burnt, the fish no longer spiked them, and the salt in the air no longer smarted in their cuts and bruises.

They were dropped at the port in Libreville, Gabon.

They said their goodbyes. Emilo had tears in his eyes. Phoebe kissed Emilo on the cheek; Don shook the strong hand. They were all very sad. Don and Phoebe really did not want to leave Emilo. The shoulders sloped on the big man. They exchanged waves until Emilo and the fishing boat was a smudge in the blue sea.

Don and Phoebe cried for a long time. And the void Emilo left they knew would never be filled.

At Pakito Lounge they met an American and his English wife. They turned down a chance to shoot pool, instead they sat down at a table. To save money Don and Phoebe drank

Djino. The English wife spoke excellent French and so she ordered drinks. The American and his English wife wanted to go and dance, but Don and Phoebe said they were exhausted.

"We hitchhiked once, a very long time ago, when we were young and foolish, from Valparaiso, Indiana, USA, to Ushuaia, Argentina," said the American.

Don and Phoebe did their best to dissuade the American from telling them about the journey, but the American was very persistent and had to have his way. His English wife smiled and ordered more drinks. Don and Phoebe missed Emilo and the sea more than ever. They slouched and fought boredom and sleep.

"Short on money we bought enough food for the trip and a tent with two sleeping bags. We caught the South Shore at Beverley Shores into Chicago. The hitchhiking from Chicago to Texas was easy. A truck out of Chicago and from outside of Chicago took a ride from two college kids that were going to watch Loyola play Kansas. From Kansas we had five lifts, from Kansas to Denver, from Denver to Oklahoma City, from Oklahoma City to Little Rock, from Little Rock to New Orleans, from New Orleans to Houston; we were stuck in Houston for three days and partied for those three days, a bus from Houston to Galveston. We caught a boat in Galveston. We were dropped off on the shore of Coatzacoalcos. From Coatzacoalcos we walked to Villahermosa. A truck took us to Belmopan City. We caught the train from Belmopan City to Panama City. Out of curiosity we decided to visit Valparaiso, Chile. On our way along E-71 we stopped at Putaendo and watched a bullfight. During the excitement a mother dropped her baby and the bull impaled the baby and cut the baby in half. It was an epiphany. I only wish I could have captured the moment on camera. A gambling man told us he would take us to Rionegro, Colombia. In the back of his truck he had thickets of velame and mandacarus. What he did not tell us was that under the thickets of velame and mandacarus were the leaves of the coca plant in green plastic bags. He promised us that in Rionegro he would ask a friend to fly us south in a private airplane. A vet by the name of Harry flew us from Rionegro to Manaus. Harry was one mean son-of-a-bitch. He drank Jack Daniels and smoked thick cigars. He was on the lam. He had killed a man in Laredo over a whore. Walking along 174 a Jagunço with three horses offered to take us through the Sertão. He talked little, grunted when he was happy, and when he was drunk he showed us the places where bullets and knives had disfigured his body. Once through the Sertão, we got a ride that took us as far as Patagonia. No writer has ever captured the true beauty of Patagonia. A Gaucho without a horse became our guide. We walked, hitchhiked, and caught a bus to Ushuaia. On Perito Francisco Moreno we found cheap lodging. We said goodbye to the Gaucho. One day I am going to write a memoir."

"Please not a memoir," said Phoebe.

The American talked nonstop about the possibilities of the memoir. The American finally stopped and went to the restroom.

"We flew most of the way and the rest we were on a train," said the English wife apologetically.

The lemonade was sweet and refreshing.

They rode in the back of a truck with two huge brown hairy pigs. They were thankful the back was open and the stench was carried away. The huge brown hairy pigs were loud and hungry. Don and Phoebe tucked their feet under their bottoms.

A family was squeezed into the front of the truck, four children, a mother, and a father.

The brown hairy pigs were for clearing snakes off farms. The brown hairy pigs ate the snakes. Don feared that the brown hairy pigs would eat them too.

The man driving the truck was The King of the Pigs. He was small and had a potbelly which rested on the bottom of the wheel.

The family spoke French. The children kept turning around and smiling and waving at Don and Phoebe. The mother would look now and again and smile diffidently.

The King of the Pigs was going to Fougamou. The King of the Pigs was a very important man. There were many snakes.

In Tchibanga they got sick. They were febrile and were as porous as sponges. Malaria had finally caught up to them.

Don and Phoebe were covered in welts from mosquito bites that they had scratched into bloody holes.

The room smelt of verdigris. The smell came from the exposed copper pipes.

A Norwegian doctor visited them in their motel. He was a tall man with lapis lazuli eyes and blond hair. His soft voice was pleasant after the engines of lorries, cars and motorbikes. They were too embarrassed to explain to him why they had to get to South Africa. They lied and said they were traveling for fun and adventure. He said that he had a friend that would fly them to Namibia; the friend would be transporting medicine in a small aeroplane.

"So what are you, hippies?" asked Kristian.

"I suppose so, yes," said Phoebe, gingerly nodding her sweat covered head.

"I hate hippies," said Kristian.

In the mornings he visited for half an hour on his way to the hospital. Don recuperated quicker than Phoebe. Kristian brought Cassava heavy cakes. He would sit in the only chair. Phoebe had to stay in bed; Don would sit on the window ledge.

Kristian and Don would eat and drink coffee while Phoebe tried to stop her knees from knocking.

Phoebe didn't feel up to talking, but she could not help herself when they started to talk about her book, the one thing that could induce her to talk was her book. Kristian was very interested. Don looked out of the window and followed a line of gulls that cut across the blue sky.

Phoebe started. She hurried on fearful of interruption or being thwarted, unafraid of lethargy. Don looked. Kristian wanted to stop Phoebe, but thought it best to wait. "A product of the epoch a moment of prodigious scientific research, religion, philosophy, education, optics, photography, writing, inventions. Born in Jedburgh, December 11, 1781"- Phoebe almost choked on the date - "he was recognized as a child prodigy. Constructed a telescope when only ten years old. Close observation, unceasing inquiry, and a scientific proclivity. Married Juliet McPherson. He constructed a lens of great diameter out of one piece of glass by cutting out the central parts in successive ridges like stair steps. Born an apparatus of then-unequaled power - the polyzonal lens - a lens constructed by building it on several circular segments. Which created light-stabs of brilliance that could pierce far into the night." Phoebe stopped to breathe. Her head collapsed into the pillows. She was sweating profusely. She looked as though sleep was too much.

"I think that should be enough for today," said Kristian.

Phoebe was red in the face, her neck and arms candle wax white, the patina of sweat glistened, she was blowing hard.

As always there was a strong smell of coffee and bread. Phoebe could only smell her sweat and the osmotic sheets, heavy and damp.

"It must have been like LSD and as addictive as any opiate," said Don trying to help the conversation.

Kristian groaned and sat back down.

"That first time must have been like traveling through space," said Don. He had never read Phoebe's book. He thought the book was about shopping.

"The kaleidoscope transcends any drug in its ability to transport the mind into the realms of higher consciousness," said Phoebe.

Kristian stood up. He looked very upset.

"The hippies and other radicals have a lot to answer for. The indigenous people of the Americas have witnessed the ramification of this abuse, misuse of their holy peyote by hippies and other radicals; they too are now considered criminals for using the religious peyote," said Kristian.

"The kaleidoscope is a paradigm of innocence, an innocence that has truly been lost, in the same way," said Phoebe.

"What should have been an epoch of great advancements turned out to be a breeding ground for consumers addicted to greed. These sophisticated kids of the void, went inwards, but missed the portal that would have led them to transcendentalism, to a higher collectiveness. Imagine what could have happened. Instead they stroked their egos, their vanity, through this journey they abandoned the collective, and decided to stand alone. Stand in queues with credit cards waiting for the latest wonder," said Kristian.

"The kaleidoscope as with many other things has been reduced to a toy, a plaything, to be used once and thrown away," said Phoebe.

Don watched the virga over the buildings sway and hold the sunlight. It was a soporific picture.

Kristian sat down and sipped his coffee.

"As the hand turns, as the light travels from mirror to mirror, as the light passes through the colored particles, down the tube, as the light travels from the optic nerve to the visual cortex, as light becomes electro-chemical impulses, the kaleidoscope allows possibilities where there were impossibilities," said Phoebe.

Don scratched his head. The malaria had slowed him down. He wanted to catch up to Kristian and Phoebe, but he was two steps behind, and fatigued.

"The kaleidoscope stands as a symbol of what could have been, as Neil Armstrong's moon walk is the apex of man's dreams. Somewhere between Brunel's Great Western

Railway and the computer we veered. Somehow the inventor became salesman. One could never imagine David Brewster standing on a soapbox flogging his wares, in a panic to please shareholders, on a billboard advertising his kaleidoscope. The kaleidoscope was never his, it was ours," said Phoebe.

Don assented with a nod of his head.

Kristian smiling, clapped loudly. Taking this as his cue, Don nodded his head and joined in with the clapping. Phoebe suddenly felt better. If she could she would have jumped out of the bed and hugged Kristian.

The malaria subsided.

Kristian drove Don and Phoebe to the airport. He handed Phoebe money and was resolute that she should keep the money and use the money to safely take them home.

Søren was as serious as Kristian. He talked about politics, religion, and diseases. The whole time he laughed only once. It was when he was talking about children.

Unfit for hitchhiking, they caught the train from Tsumeb to Gobabis. The train was slow and overcrowded. A peasant woman in many colors fed them and said a prayer for them. They thanked her with the headphones. The peasant woman tied the headphones around the neck of the chicken she was holding and walked the chicken up and down the train to roaring laughter. The headphones were worth a year's pay, but Don and Phoebe didn't tell the peasant woman. The coquettish chicken was very happy and paraded up and down kicking its feet as though its life depended upon it.

ICEBERG

j

As the iceberg drifted past the peaks that were once the Falkland Islands, death was no longer a worry, death had not been one storm away, it had entered the tent, it had not been out there, it had been all around them, close, touching, at the fastigium its cold breath had numbed their skin, it had whispered into their ears, clogged their nostrils, laid concrete upon their eyes, stolen kisses, but now death was in the past, Don and Phoebe, exhilarated, renewed, waved at the peaks peeking through the tranquil sea, a sea that had once been vexed, vociferous, derogatory, and celebrated that they were alive, that they had survived, no matter what lay ahead now, no matter what vicissitudes, no matter what trials and tribulations, they had been at their nadir, they had seen and felt what life really meant, they understood death and now life, they had seen no hope, and so now it could only get better, they were moving, moving up, moving slowly, but all the same moving, and movement meant life, more life, life meant flux, life was unambiguous, the snow, ice, screaming darkness, cold had been the concrescence, now life was something they could feel, touch, explore, life was a huge anthology, an anthology that they could fathom, each second of the day, each movement forward, no matter how infinitesimal, was as important as each hair spouting from their bodies. Luck more than obstinacy had kept them alive, but to them it did not matter, death had been real, it had been tangible, they had touched death and death had touched them and death had illuminated to them that they were living, that life meant something wonderful, death had been articulate, eloquent, clear and concise, mellifluous, the perfect teacher. Now life was more beautiful then ever, life was a whale breaking the surface of the sea, life was gulls flying overhead obstreperous and loquacious, life was a mercurial cloud changing its formation again and again unwilling to be pinned down like the butterfly for the etymologist, life was the sun and the moon and the myriad of stars, life was the undulating sea. Life had unclogged their ears, removed the curtains from their eyes, uncemented their nostrils, life had presented life as a children's book presents the apple for A. It was warm and the breeze held a hint of vegetation and as they stared out at the expanding and contracting horizons they realized that they could no longer hear the patter of penguins' feet or the puling of seals, and they laughed as only those that have stood on the precipice can laugh, they laughed loud and hard and contained in their laughter was an unambiguous joy, a real joy, they laughed and hugged and blessed the sky, the sea, and the iceberg. Only two months before they had been on the verge of death, it had been a very slow journey through moribundity. Under a porous tent they had huddled together and, unable to cry, talked weakly about their life. Over and over again they reminisced about their amazing journey. Out of the dark recesses they were able to recall moments they had thought had never been stored away for such a day. They giggled when they talked about such things as blisters, welts, red raw inner thighs, burnt skin, fever, hunger, thirst, each phenomena was a diamond extracted from the earth, a blister on the heel was as important to them as The Tower of London, or The British Library, the hue of damaged skin excited them more than Turner's hazy skies or turbulent seas, the sensation of hunger and thirst delighted them more than music or images on the television. They held on tightly as the winds buffeted their sleeping bags and they laughed at how the drone of mosquitoes had made them jump out of bed, how the wind had metamorphosed into a roaring, pugnacious loin, how ferruginous water had made them drunk, or a simple vegetable had made them delirious as though they had consumed a huge steak. In that dark biting night they relived the journey. Their minds expanded beyond the cold. They were euphoric. Hyperventilating they watched the sun give way peacefully to the moon; it was an act of great affability. The surrounding ice mountains gradually disintegrated until all that was left for the eye to discern were rippling lines scratched into the darkening sky. Black embellishments filled with mendacity approached turning into birds, cars, youths with clubs and knives, into the landlord, but to only fade into a monotonous drone of a city vivified with untranslatable utterances. The sky morphed into the sea, soft, undulating, a sea filled with whales, sharks, and seahorses. The infinity of the sky stirred emotions that subsided only with thoughts of mundane irrelevance. A violent streak of orange shot across the mass of black, the orange softly, slowly spread, illuminating unfathomable creatures, breathing, moving. On knees they watched the moon give way to the sun. It had to, it had no alternative. The sea was a mass of gold. The sky was transparent. "If heaven existed and you were welcomed would you enter if all your secrets had to be revealed?" asked Phoebe. There were some things that Don did want to forget but Phoebe helped him and made him laugh. Unable to cope with the desolation Don decided to shoot himself in the mouth with the flare gun the drug addict scientist had sold to them. Trembling with fear and cold the flare gun would not fit into his mouth. He held his lips as wide as they would go and placed the flare gun on the tip of his bottom lip. The weight was too much. Before he could pull the trigger Phoebe caught him. "What you doing sweetpea?" asked Phoebe. Don collapsed onto the ice. It was snowing. He rolled up into the fetal position. The flare gun fell out of his gloved hand. "We are free," said Phoebe. She could not believe what she was witnessing. They had finally arrived at the other end. They had washed off death and all signs of death, in cool pools of water they had washed off the embellishments, they had removed the decubitus that had stuck to their body like the barnacles that cling to rocks. They had fought and won. Don nodded his head. Phoebe picked up the flare gun. "Why would you want to leave when we have all this?" said Phoebe. With her hand she illuminated their ice kingdom. Don's eye traveled over the white ice, over the blue ice and dropped over where the ice was smooth, dangerous and transparent and glided over a sea that was not impassive to death. Don mumbled something inaudible. Phoebe laughed and helped Don to his feet. "This is our Castle and we are the Kings," said Phoebe. They hugged. Phoebe whispered love into Don's ear. They went back to the tent. It was a sad memory but with Phoebe's help Don was able to see the absurdity of his actions. He laughed as he remembered trying to force the flare gun between his damaged lips, he blushed as he remembered Phoebe standing perplexed before him with her gloved hands on her disappearing hips. "I miss my dad," said Don. He was too cold, too sleepy, too exhausted to cry. "I know you do," said Phoebe and she pushed the tip of her nose to Don's. Too sleepy to move she left the tip of her nose adhered to Don's. Don's diaphanous warm breath kept her lips warm. As the wind hammered the outside of the tent like a bunch of youths with nothing better to do than spoil the peace and tranquility of a night of camping they vowed never to give up the ghost, they would be steadfast, they would fight death, they would be obdurate and stare death down. It was a joyous moment, as the tent was battered, as the wind careened through the apertures, the snow obfuscated, as the sea roared, they glowed, for they had decided to live life, they would no longer dwell in the doldrums closer to death, they were euphoric, as the cold bit them with the teeth of wild dogs, as the wind punched and kicked them with the violence of the landlord and his gang of hoodied youths, as the snow turned to rain and drenched them, they bloomed and felt vigorous, their thoughts were fecund, their dreams iridescent. With their eyes closed they traveled along the same roads, they sat in their favorite beer garden, they walked up and down the streets they had known, but the streets were different, all menace and violence had been whitewashed away, as had the dog excrement from off the leveled pavements. They pictured the landlord's face and the mad dog on his neck as he entered the flat with the missing television. They laughed at his red face and the bulging veins in his neck that turned the mad dog into a whining penguin. They removed all the lorries, buses, cars and motorcars from the roads they had traveled; they whitewashed the red lights out of Amsterdam; they unpopulated the hotels of Antwerp; they invited Emilo to walk with them through Père Lachaise Cemetery; they unleashed the bulls and allowed the bulls to have free reign and use their horns to cut the people that had mocked and teased them; they played cards in the bar as Emilo shouted at the sleeping barman "¡Despierta!" They laughed and joked with Emilo. They dined on good, rich food and drank fine wines, hard liquor, and good beer. They danced to wild music and allowed the night to shroud them. They created a new London. They started with one square. It was large. The square needed a public building and so they built a public building where the public could go and have tea and toast. They built four roads, North, South, East, and West. They named the roads Accra, Libreville, Annobón, and Riaba. They lined the roads with the buildings they could remember and housed the buildings with the faces they could recreate. Emilo would be President and BadBoy the Prime Minister. Don and Phoebe would live at the top of a hill in a villa that had huge windows so that they could see verdant hills, tall trees, and birds flying through an azure sky, and beyond the verdant hills and tall trees the sea lambent with gold would fill the air with mellifluous song. "We've done it," said Phoebe leaving the tent. Don followed. They took off the goggles and gloves they had bought from the drug addict scientist in Cape Town. They remembered him, they felt so sorry for him, they lived above him in the motel, he had sold them all of his gear, all his special clothing; the cold would have finished them off without the special clothing, he didn't need the special clothing, he had locked himself in his room and injected drugs into his system. Their second piece of luck was fishing tackle that Emilo had tucked surreptitiously into Phoebe's rucksack. It was fundamental stuff but it worked wonderfully. They caught plenty of fish. They cooked the fish the way Emilo had showed them. The fish was good. Their third piece of luck was a huge sheet of tin. To get the sheet of tin up onto the iceberg they had to dismantle their tent and use the rope to haul it up. They folded the sheet of tin and placed it over the tent. By the time the sun had passed over them the tin was very hot. It was so hot they could melt ice for water, dry clothing and slow bake fish. "We should eat," said Don. Phoebe nodded her head. The peaks were so nice to look at. They were like jewels upon a crown. The sun had turned them purple. Don and Phoebe had more food than they could eat. A whale that had been killed by a Japanese whaling ship had escaped being processed and the sea presented the whale to Don and Phoebe. Emilo had been right, they had been good to the sea and now the sea was being good to them. They cut up the whale with sad hearts, Phoebe cried, while Don hacked through the whale. And so Don and Phoebe had oil for their fire and blubber to smear over their tent and food to keep them going. With the whale bones they constructed a fence with the hope the fence would keep out the polar bears. Although they had not seen any polar bears, they liked the idea of the whale bones keeping out imaginary polar bears. They had seen the Japanese whaling ship in the distance. And one night they thought that the Japanese whaling ship was attacking their home with their water cannons. They hid under their sleeping bags and prayed that the sheet of tin would hold. In the morning they woke to the sound of pitter patter. They went outside and found that they had not been attacked by the Japanese whaling ship. It was raining. Never had they felt so happy to see the rain. They hollered and danced in the rain. And although the rain was cold and the wind was cold they removed their headgear, they removed their gloves, and they removed their coats. After the rain the sun shone blindingly. Their skin burnt and their hair was blanched. The nights were as hot as the days.

When the iceberg drifted past the peaks that were once the Falkland Islands it was four acres. The plateau was good for them to build upon. The ice was a phosphorescent blue during the night and so they were able to work both night and day. Don and Phoebe worked hard. They chipped away at the ice. They remodeled the ice and remolded the ice. The sea was indeed plentiful. From the sea they had gathered enough material to build. Don and Phoebe cut up the sheet of tin and used other materials that they had plucked from the sea and built a Geodesic dome. Don thanked the landlord for making him read the book on architecture. Phoebe was impressed with Don's skill and memory. "Now I know why I love you," said Phoebe. Don blushed. Together they worked, shoulder to shoulder, neither letting the other one down; there was no shirking, no excuses, no complaining, no moaning. They found that they enjoyed the work; their bodies had never felt so good. They lined the inside of the dome with fur coats that they found in three plastic containers floating in the sea. The Geodesic dome worked wonderfully and kept them dry and safe.

They were shocked at the things they had plucked from the sea: a latrine, a shower, a couch, a table, a box of candles of varying scents, windows, a door and deckchairs. They had found boxes floating with televisions, radios, computers, and other electronics, but these things they allowed the sea to keep.

They sat on the deckchairs and watched ships sail past their home. A cruise ship tried to communicate with them but the wind obstructed any chance of communication. The people waved and threw objects. Don and Phoebe escaped into their home. The sound of banging scared them. After ten minutes the banging stopped. They went out and found bottles of beer and hard liquor scattered all around their home. "I thought they were trying to kill us," said Don. He stooped down and picked up a bottle of champagne. "We have to stop being fearful of everything. We have to stand up tall and refuse to kneel. We have faced down death, we can do anything," said Phoebe. Don nodded his head and opened up a bottle of champagne. He took a swig while Phoebe picked up the cork. "We must not waste a single thing," said Phoebe. Don handed Phoebe the bottle of champagne. "The last time I drank champagne was when my book was accepted. The champagne was awful," said Phoebe. She looked sad. The book had been a huge disappointment. "That's good champagne," said Don watching Phoebe. She took a long, unladylike swig. "Yes, it is damn good champagne," said Phoebe and she belched.

The moon laid before them a trajectory, a road which they would follow. The iceberg slowly drifted and the sea hardly caused a fuss. The sea was never the same sea, the sea was as mercurial as the weather, as mysterious as the night sky, as beautiful as any dream. The sea was perplexing, elusive, the sea for Phoebe was many things and each of these things were different from what Don thought the sea should be, but both loved the sea. Don constantly praised the sea, whereas Phoebe now and again told off the sea. Don and Phoebe had never been so happy, so close, so free. They stood near the edge of the iceberg, the wind nothing more than a brushstroke and they eyed the path laid out by the moon as they had eyed the road as it stretched out along the even landscape until it vanished. "I really thought we were going to perish," said Don. He opened a bottle of beer and passed it to Phoebe. "Let's sit down," said Phoebe. They sat in the deckchairs and watched dolphins as they entertained. "I had faith," said Phoebe. She sipped her beer. "After everything we had been through I just had a feeling we would make it," said Phoebe. "I always wanted to be in a happy story," said Don. The dolphins were very busy. The sea was thriving with life.

Don and Phoebe created an upstairs area where they could sleep. Their love-making was long and full of bliss. Don removed some of the tin spherical panels and replaced them with clear plastic so that they could lie in bed after their love-making and stare up into the starry night sky.

Specks of life infiltrated their island. Where the ice had melted rock protruded. An incongruity of green appeared in patches. Nodes of life sparkled. Moss grew prodigiously.

One morning they found a car. They pushed the car until it was outside their home. "We could never have afforded a car such as this," said Phoebe. It was a big German car. It was black and very expensive. There had been much water damage. It brought back memories of the car Phoebe had bought in a flurry of excitement. In the windows they saw their reflections. They had changed. The superfluity of the modern world had been cut away; their once pallid complexions had been painted over by the sun. "Let's get in," said Don. He opened the door and jumped in. Phoebe sat in the passenger seat. The leather seats squeaked and cold water poured down their legs. Don grabbed the wheel and put the car into gear. "So where do you want to go?" asked Don. Phoebe looked at all the new stuff that made the car so expensive. "Let's just stay here," said Phoebe. Don turned off the imaginary purring engine and laced his hands behind his head. "You know what they say about a Jag," said Don and his seat fell back. He had a nefarious smile upon his face. "This is not a Jag," said Phoebe smiling proudly, climbing out of the car. Before Don had a chance to bring his plan to fruition Phoebe climbed out of the car. "We have work to do, silly boy, work," said Phoebe. The car came in handy when Don and Phoebe wanted to sunbathe after washing themselves in one of the small pools of warm water that were appearing as the ice melted and the rock underneath became more prominent. They were shocked at how much rock was under the ice. The rock close to the house was smooth; at the edge the rock was craggy. Vegetation clung to the rock and it blossomed prodigiously. Flowers appeared as they drifted past Argentina. The flowers were beautiful. Don and Phoebe had never seen such an array of colours. Bushes and fruit trees grew where birds had dropped seeds. They were amazed at the diverse flora that appeared. "What the hell is this?" asked Don, holding up a rather strange fruit. Phoebe shook her head. Don turned it around and marveled at its design. It was intricate and beautiful. Don and Phoebe were in awe. "Give it a name," said Phoebe. Don laughed. He tossed another of the fruit to Phoebe. She squeezed it. "My little ulul," said Don and he bit into the unripe fruit. "Adam never gets the credit he deserves," said Phoebe. "Not bad," said Don. He expectorated seeds. "Old man Adam looking back must have felt slightly perturbed. As his bones creaked and groaned he must have been saddened by all the time wasted. As his teeth fell out and his hair thinned and turned to silver he must have wept for all the words he had given birth to. As his legs buckled and his hearing faded and his eyes clogged he must have cursed God. After all had he not spent the same amount of time and energy creating? The naming of everything was a feat just as worthy as creating the heavens, the stars, the sea, the land and all that was on the land," composed Phoebe.

They had never been so comfortable. They spent their mornings working, after work they sat in the deckchairs and drank and ate and watched the expanding and contracting horizons, at night they lay together.

The sea filled with life showed that life and death are married and could never be divorced and they cherished this.

Phoebe remembered poetry and snippets of literature. Don talked about the paintings he could remember and loved. They sang tunes with made-up lyrics; they invented foreign words for the arias they could remember, they reenacted the movies they had seen. "I am going to a write a story," said Phoebe. Her head was brimming with stories that she had picked up along her great journey. She wanted to write about the ladies who sold vegetables in Cape Coast. She wanted to tell the world about the iceberg. "Without a typewriter it will be hard. You haven't even a pen or paper," said Don. Phoebe smiled. "I'll do it in my head and when I get something it will already be done," said Phoebe. Don liked the idea. "I'll do the same with painting," said Don.

As the land receded and the sea became everything they got drunk. They sat on the deckchairs and drank hard liquor, something they had never done before. It had been Phoebe's idea. The sky was clear and the sea tranquil. It felt as though they were sitting in a beer garden, a place were no children were crying or being rambunctious, where dogs were allowed and the barmaid brought water in a bowl for the dog. Don and Phoebe missed their dog. "I wish we had dog here now," said Phoebe. Don chipped some ice from a little mound that was between them and put the chips of ice into their cups. He poured the hard liquor over the chipped ice. "Cheers," said Phoebe. She lifted up her glass so that the sun could illuminate the ice. "Bottoms up," said Don. They sat in silence and awe and watched a long winged albatross turn into an irascible gull. "This liquor is very strong," said Phoebe. She started to cry. "I am so happy," said Phoebe. Don leaned over and wrapped an arm around Phoebe. She stopped crying and sipped her drink. She smiled. Don removed his arm and placed a kiss on Phoebe's shoulder. She sipped her drink. It was strong and she had to grimace to vent. Don refilled his glass. Now that Phoebe had a smile on her face he went with the liquor she was drinking. He took a sip and also vented with a grimace. They laughed freely.

As the iceberg slowly, very slowly rotated, it crossed the Atlantic Ocean. The sea had never seemed so big and vast. For months they did not see land. As rare as their fights a tanker would sail by, it would blow its horn and the sailors would wave. Sometimes the sailors would throw things, food, hard liquor, coats, shoes, but Phoebe and Don had no need for coats and shoes. The sailors were always happy to see Don and Phoebe. The sailors always tried to communicate, but they spoke in many languages and Don and Phoebe could only speak English. The iceberg ostensibly broke up the monotony of their journey. "I really think they like us," said Don. Phoebe nodded her head. They liked the fact that people liked them.

It rained for a full month. The air was no longer abrasive, the salt in the air lightened. As the iceberg passed Sierra Leone many trees bloomed and presented many exotic fruits. Don and Phoebe cultivated their garden. They watched the cucumber plant sprawl and were amazed how it gripped onto anything it could with its stringy tentacles and how it produced so quickly its cucumbers. The tomato plants grew tall and the tomatoes were juicy. The garden produced jalapeños, green and red peppers, the trees fruited and there were apples, lemons, and pears. There were berries, black and red. Wild strawberries clung to the rocks. They found okra and were very excited. They had the okra and thought of BadBoy and the cave paintings.

The sea was indeed a junkyard. They built upon the dome, a games-room, outdoor patio with expensive furniture. They plucked from the sea a street lamp and stood it up next to the car. They got umbrellas from a container and so were able to sit in the shade. They replaced their deckchairs with fancy beach furniture that had been made in China and was being shipped to Miami. "Tell me about the Kaleidoscope," said Don. He was slightly drunk. They had just had a meal of fish, okra, and a fruit salad. They were drinking cocktails. The sea current was taking them back over the Atlantic Ocean towards North America. "Kaleidoscope derives from the Ancient Greek *καλός* meaning beauty, beautiful, *εἶδος*, form, shape and *σκόπιο*, tool for examination. Translation: observer of beautiful forms," said Phoebe. Don felt very guilty. "I wish I had read the book. I am very sorry that I didn't support you as much as I should have," said Don. Phoebe smiled and stroked Don upon the face. "You will never know just how much you have supported me," said Phoebe. They exchanged a smile. "Tell me more," said Don. He wasn't feigning, he really wanted to know and Phoebe felt very happy. "The colored light inside the kaleidoscope is God as the light having passed through the stained glass window of a cathedral is God." She froze. She looked around her. "The kaleidoscope contains God. I thought you didn't believe in God," said Don. "I don't believe in God with the white beard and blue eyes but I believe in that God," said Phoebe pointing to the sun. Don understood. He really wished he had read the book.

Curiosity expands; it reaches into the darkness, the recesses. The worlds don't simply disappear. They fade softly like snow. Isolation distorts time like the way the sun creates shadows. Their shadows traveled over the sea creating lands new and foreign. Thoughts fell. The fall is not over quickly. They drift down like snowflakes, twirling, swirling. As they fall there is a moment, a point, an arrowhead say, where they are no longer falling downwards, nor are they going up, they are suspended, motionless; it is as though gravity has given up. Orchids grew bountiful. The sea kept giving. The sea was full of discarded stuff. Miles and miles of flotsam and jetsam journeyed across the ocean. Don and Phoebe played with kites that they had found in a plastic box. The earth had stopped spinning. The wind was gentle. Don watched Phoebe run pulled along by her kite. Her hair was matted, twisted, a twig was entangled. Weeds and flowers were pressed hard against her dew dappled ankles. Don was amazed by the swirl of colors, purples, bright reds, and glorious yellows, so many different shades of blue and green. Phoebe glided over the rock, over grass, over the ice. The winds brushed back her hair. Her thighs were salmon pink. Phoebe felt no pain as the bottom of her feet pressed into the rocks, into the stones, into the ice. When she laughed she rolled and exposed her breasts. She had small breasts. They were white. He liked her small white breasts that made her nipples look so healthy so ready for the lips of a baby. He ran a finger down her spine. She felt soft. He liked the softness. It felt good running a finger down along the spine, feeling each protruding knuckle. She sighed. She rested her head on the pillow made of feathers. He stopped just before the point where the coccyx slightly protruded. Time had evaporated.

A Brazilian fisherman not lost but adrift told them that the world was underwater. The old man pointed to the sky and said God had spoken to him. He said his name was Noah. He spoke many languages. They didn't believe him. "The sea has reclaimed," he said. They laughed and exchanged fruit for fish.

They had the fish with a bottle of Romanée Conti. They cooked it the old method, the way Emilo had showed them how to cook fish. "It could have happened," said Don. Phoebe bit her bottom lip. She looked worried. They had noticed the sea-level rising. At first they feared that the ice underneath them was melting. But after many days they surmised that the sea-level was indeed rising. "All those people, all that land, all those beautiful buildings, all that history," said Phoebe. Don emptied his glass and poured more Romanée Conti. "The people would not have noticed. It would have happened slowly," said Don. Phoebe emptied her glass. "What like Athens and Rome?" said Phoebe. Don was confused and so shrugged. He refilled their glasses from a second bottle of Romanée Conti.

The iceberg passed what was once Cuba. There were many sharks; this was because of the abundance of food. Carrion floated on the sea. The carrion seeped into the sea. Don and Phoebe stopped sunbathing and drinking in their deckchairs. They stayed in the dome. They fixed up the rooms. They laid a wooden floor. Constructed walls and fixed doors. They put up shelves and even though they did not possess books they built bookshelves. Phoebe wanted a back door so Don and Phoebe cut a hole in the dome and fixed a back door. Phoebe said that she wanted to have a back garden. She removed the wild vegetation and planted flowers. Phoebe's garden blossomed. Humming birds, bees, wasps, and flies visited Phoebe's back garden.

Florida was nothing more than a sliver of land.

A dog floating on an advertisement for the Hilton Hotel appeared on the horizon. They climbed down the stairs that they constructed. The stairs went around the iceberg and descended slowly. They used the stairs so they could swim. Phoebe had to teach Don how to swim. He was a hopeless swimmer. Phoebe was patient and did her best. The dog's name was Spencer. They fed the dog fish. They were all very happy. At night Spencer slept at the foot of the bed. The dog was vivacious and played all the time. Don and Phoebe enjoyed having Spencer around. Spencer was full of fun.

The summer was long. It felt as though they had missed many winters. Most of the ice had melted from the top of the iceberg. They worked hard cultivating the forest that grew around them, reshaping the rock, fixing their home. When the sea was tranquil they swam in the warm sea.

Through the dense fog lighthouses more numerous than stars shimmered.

A yachting boat sailed lazily by. It was a huge gleaming monstrosity. It reminded Don and Phoebe of a floating disco. The people on board were more than happy and drinking champagne. They were having a wonderful time, they were almost naked. They were laughing and some were dancing. "Ennui is a thing of the past," said Phoebe. A baldheaded man red in the face caught their attention. Don and Phoebe were fixated upon his white teeth. "You're famous," he said. Incredulous, Don and Phoebe feigned laughter. "Famous?" said Phoebe. The fat man held out his arms akimbo. It was as though he wanted to give the iceberg a hug. He looked very silly, sunburnt, gold Speedos, white even teeth and bald. "Yes, famous," said the fat man. "The kids love you. You are a phenomenon. The kids absolutely love you. The kids can't get enough of you. The kids idolize you. You're all over the kids' computers, television, magazines. The kids love you." A blonde, tanned woman in large sunglasses tried to drag him away. Her golden bikini glowed in the sun. She had huge breasts. "You are famous. Everybody is talking about you. You're all over the place." Finally the woman got him to budge. "You're the talk of the town. Although which town I don't know." He laughed at his own joke and followed the woman.

Don and Phoebe had to light fires so that the iceberg would not collide with yachts and boats. The sea was full of yachts and boats. Everybody wanted to speak to Don and Phoebe. There was a constant cheer in the air. Don and Phoebe never got sick and tired of waving and yelling and saying thank you. A helicopter hovered and lowered a reporter. Don and Phoebe were unsure how to handle the reporter. He asked many questions and they tried to answer the questions. He used a computer but he had a pen and notebook. Seeing how hard he was working Don poured him a drink. They went into the dome and carried on the questions and answers. "You could get a great book deal out of this," said the reporter. He was very young and very, very trendy. "Could I?" said Phoebe. The reporter nodded his head and finished his drink. "A memoir, they are all the rage now, your book would fit in perfectly with the zeitgeist," said the reporter. He looked as though he knew what he was talking about. He rolled up his multicoloured shirt sleeve and showed them a tattoo of a famous quote. "I could write a memoir," said Phoebe. The reporter removed the pages he had used from the notebook and handed the notebook to Phoebe. Phoebe thanked him but she would have preferred the computer. "Thank you so much," said Phoebe. She showed the notebook to Don. "You'll need a pen," said the reporter. The reporter spent the night and in the morning the helicopter picked him up. Don and Phoebe were sad to see the reporter leave. "We shall see each other again," said the reporter. The helicopter upset Don's vegetable garden and fruit trees and Phoebe's back garden but they didn't care. "I hope," said Phoebe. "At your book launch," said the reporter.

Paparazzi filmed Don and Phoebe sunbathing naked and drinking too much. A kid handed Phoebe the magazine. Don was on the front cover. He was naked. The magazine made fun of his superfluous fat. "I think you should start wearing shorts," said Phoebe. Don cut the legs off his jeans. "God I only hope they are not comparing us to Adam and Eve," said Don. "Yes that would be rather boring and simple," said Phoebe. Don showed Phoebe his new shorts. They looked awful. Phoebe promised herself that once her memoir was made into a movie she would buy Don some better shorts, designer and very fashionable. "We are Phoebe and Don," said Don. He would also get new teeth.

"Yes," said Phoebe.

Most of North Carolina, Virginia and West Virginia had been reclaimed by the sea.

The lighthouses turned out to be skyscrapers.

The iceberg slowed and they bathed in the hot weather, the sea hardly moved, it was dappled with lambent flecks of golden sunlight.

Birds, ducks, peacocks, swans and other wildlife invaded the iceberg.

The iceberg drifted in a cloud of fog. Don and Phoebe were cut off from the world and this made them sad. They pined for the people on the yachts and boats. They worked but not much, they pared back the wildlife, they uprooted plants. Anything onerous was left. They worked for half an hour each day. The rest of the day they drank to douse their sadness.

The iceberg was rocked, the dome lost some of its panels, windows smashed, and the front door and back door came away from the jambs. The street lamp was slanted, the car had moved. Trees were uprooted; rock shot up and towered over the dome creating a shadow that cooled the rooms in the dome. The last of the ice fell away.

They had stopped moving.

They looked over the side and down upon the top of a huge head.

They were no longer floating in the sea.

Their home had been impaled upon the flames of the Statue of Liberty.

"I've always wanted to live in New York City," said Phoebe as she placed her new typewriter upon a writing table that had a gold plaque screwed into the top which said the table had once belonged to Mark Twain.

Please review this book wherever possible, and help support the author and independent publishing. Thank you.

Also by Honest Publishing

Homegirl!
Ryder Collins

Jazz
Jéanpaul Ferro

Nothing Doing
Willie Smith

The Killing of a Bank Manager
Paul Kavanagh

The Wooden Tongue Speaks
Bogdan Tiganov

Wedding Underwear for Mermaids
Linda Ann Strang

Find out more at www.honestpublishing.com